The Bosun's Secret

Phil Carradice

PONT

First Impression—2000

ISBN 1 85902 719 9

This book is published with the support of the
Arts Council of Wales.

Printed in Wales at
Gomer Press, Llandysul, Ceredigion

For Trudy,
who took Nat to her heart.

Chapter One

JANUARY 1870

A cold rain hammered in from the west, driving down onto the mud flats and whipping at the rigging of the schooners moored in Cardiff Bay. It was not a night to be out.

The streets of the great city seemed to be almost empty. A few last shoppers clutched their meagre purchases to their chests and hurried home to the warmth and security of their families. The occasional reveller lurched unsteadily across mud-stained, dripping pavements heading for the nearest tavern or coffee house. Nothing else moved.

The only sound came from the wind which howled like a million banshee warriors around the corners of the buildings. Then, faintly at first but with growing intensity, came the rapid clip of a horse's hooves. Presently a carriage, drawn by a single panting pony, came into view. The driver was huddled deep inside a canvas cape and the blinds across the windows were drawn shut.

Inside the carriage Nat Thomas shivered and tried to pull the grey blanket more tightly around his shoulders.

'Keep still, boy!'

An elbow jabbed harshly into his ribs and Nat slid away to the far side of the carriage seat. He snarled at the man – dark-suited and sombre – who had been his companion ever since the court had pronounced sentence. Already, and without real reason, Nat hated him. The man's gaze rested on Nat briefly, contemptuously, then he looked away. He reached out and raised the window blind by an inch or two.

From his corner of the carriage Nat squinted through the gap and was able to pick out buildings which gleamed wet with rain. Here and there, above the skyline or between warehouses, he saw the occasional mast or spar of a great ship. Then the man let the blind drop and he could see no more.

Frowning, Nat thought back to the events of the past few days. He could not really remember how they had caught him. It had happened two, maybe three, days ago and had receded into a blur in his mind. He remembered standing at his usual pitch outside the station in Newport. The London express had just rolled into the platform in a cloud of steam and smoke and passengers were beginning to hurry out of the long grey building. He had held out his hand and adopted his usual hang-dog expression; then the policeman's baton had caught him across the side of his head. The blow had flung him to the ground and dulled his senses. He remembered little else.

He knew that he had spent time in a police cell but that was all. This morning, however, this morning he remembered well enough. The high-ceilinged, white-painted room, he remembered, and faces, row upon row of faces. Policemen, magistrates, spectators in the public gallery – the room seemed to be full of people. And in particular he remembered the hatred in all their eyes.

'Vagrancy is a crime,' the chief magistrate had

intoned, leaning forward across the bench. 'A foul crime which degrades our town. We will not have vagrants and beggars here!'

Nat had sniffed and almost smiled – almost but not quite. He knew dozens of homeless boys, boys just like himself, boys who lived rough and scavenged a living in the docklands of south Wales. Vagrants? There were enough vagrants here to make an army.

But he said nothing and let the magistrate ramble on. In the end they had given him a blanket to cover his nakedness and sent him off with this man in a hansom carriage.

He had had no food. That was not unusual; Nat was used to going days without eating. He tried to remember when his belly had last felt really full. It was impossible. He had known no comfort or warmth for as long as he could remember – not since his mother had died, five or six years ago.

Despite everything, despite the long years of brutality and pain, at that moment the thought of his mother was too close for comfort. Best not to think of it. He sniffed and sat up in his seat. The man alongside him looked up suddenly and banged on the roof of the carriage with his cane.

'Turn here!' he called. 'The ship is a few hundred yards down river.'

Industrial School, the magistrate had said, that was where he was bound; sentenced to five years in an Industrial School for vagrancy and begging. Nat had stared at him, not really comprehending. He had not felt fear – fear was a luxury he could barely afford. He had coped with adversity for years and this, he thought, was just one more problem to overcome.

'You need discipline, boy,' the magistrate had said, 'a good dose of control and hard punishment. Idle loafers like you deserve nothing less.'

The threat did not worry Nat. He would not stay long at their stupid school, he would escape as soon as he was able. Yet there was something, something vicious and vengeful in the way the man spoke. So Nat was, at least, suddenly wary.

'The Industrial School Ship *Havannah* is moored in Cardiff. They'll take care of you there, boy.'

The man smiled, grimly, and Nat had the sudden impression that he could have said more, that what he really wanted to add was the phrase 'And may God have mercy on your soul!'

Now, the carriage drew up suddenly, the horse snorting and shaking its mane in the driving rain. Nat's companion opened the door and climbed out.

'Wait here,' he told the driver. 'I won't be long.'

Reaching back into the carriage he seized Nat by the shoulder and dragged him out into the darkness.

'Move,' he snarled, raising a huge black umbrella to keep off the rain. 'Down that path.'

A vicious push sent Nat sprawling full length in the mud. He scrambled to his feet and for a moment thought of running, of taking to his heels and disappearing into the night. The path was narrow, however, bordered by a huge black fence and the dark-suited man stood between him and freedom. Fair enough – his chance would come. He trotted easily down the path towards the river. The wind and rain were like ice on his bare legs.

It was too dark to see much but he knew that the river was close. He could smell the stale stench of mud and

10

once, as the path curved to the left, he saw the masts of many ships moored out in the bay.

Soon, however, the dark bulk of what seemed to be a wall loomed up in front of him. To the left and to the right the wall swept away into the darkness. Bright yellow pinpricks of light were dotted here and there along its length.

Nat stopped and stared. The wall was enormous, vertical and black like the heaps of coal or slag which littered the docks and railway yards of south Wales. It was made of wood, covered with tar, and seemed to soar upwards for ever. Even in his wonder Nat knew this was not just a wall. It was more substantial than that. It seemed to have a life or existence of its own. It must be a building of some type, he thought.

'What is that?' he eventually managed to gasp.

His companion came to a halt behind him. Nat could hear him breathing heavily – the man was obviously out of condition. Maybe I should have run, he thought, he would never have caught me. Now the man's hand came down on Nat's shoulder, almost as if he could sense the boy's thoughts.

'That,' he said 'is the School Ship *Havannah*. Your home for the next five years.'

Nat stared. How on earth could this be a ship? He had lived on the streets of Newport for years and was used to seeing ships in the docks or on the Channel, ships of all types and descriptions. This was like no ship he had ever seen.

She had no masts or spars or rigging of any sort. The whole of her upper deck seemed to have been roofed over, giving her as Nat had first thought, the impression of being a solid wall. More than anything she looked like a gigantic Noah's Ark, Nat decided, suddenly remembering a picture he had seen in his mother's Bible, many years before.

'That's a ship?' he stammered, shaking his head and staring. 'She goes to sea like that?'

The man's grip on his shoulders was vice-like. Nat could feel his fingers tightening, digging into his flesh.

'She won't go to sea, boy. Never again. But she'll do for you.'

They went up a narrow gangplank, balancing above the mud and filth of the river bank. Nat was used to heights, having spent half his short life crawling over the roof tops, shinning up and down drain pipes. The gangplank didn't worry him. The dark-suited man, however, clung firmly to the rope handrail and kept his eyes fixed on the side of the *Havannah* ahead of him.

'Get a move on,' he snarled, once, tripping over Nat's heels. 'You'll have us both in the river in a minute.'

Nat smiled to himself and, for a moment, considered driving his shoulder into the man's midriff and taking his luck in the mud below. Then they were at the top of the walkway, pausing before an opening which had been cut into the side of the ship. A short, squat man dressed in a sailor's jersey stood waiting for them.

'Bosun Willett, a new boy for you.'

The man called Bosun Willett inclined his head but did not speak. He was old with a white beard but his eyes, hard and deep blue, seemed to pierce right into Nat. He stood on the platform at the top of the gangplank, filling the space, leaving nobody in doubt who was in charge here.

They squeezed past the sailor into a dark chamber, which smelt heavily of paraffin and tar. After that everything seemed to happen quickly. His escort disappeared and Nat was taken below decks to an empty, echoing cabin. There he was stripped of his few ragged garments. A huge wooden tub stood in the centre of the room.

'Get in,' said Bosun Willett.

Nat glanced at the scum of dirty water which slopped around the bottom of the tub.

'But it's . . .'

A vicious blow caught him on the side of the temple and he crashed to the deck. His head swam.

'Get in,' repeated Willett.

There was no emotion in his voice. It was as if he had never laid a finger on Nat and the boy was suddenly scared. Hardened as he was to pain, Nat recognised a cold brutality in the old sailor and it was terrifying. He knew that he meant nothing to this man, that he would as soon kill him as kick him. So he climbed into the freezing water and sat shivering.

'Scrub up,' said the Bosun, throwing him a large cake of soap.

Nat did as he was told. The soap was hard as rock, smelling of carbolic, and it was difficult to make it lather in the cold water. Strangely, however, he took a simple pleasure in working at the dirt and filth which coated his thin body. Soon the scum of water at the bottom of the tub was thicker than ever and Nat was cleaner than he had been in years.

Three times Bosun Willett poured buckets of ice cold water over his head. They took Nat's breath away but he welcomed the cascade and would have sat there for hours.

'Out.'

He stood, shivering, on the wooden deck, hands clasped low to protect himself. The Bosun had disappeared and for a moment Nat wondered if he was supposed to follow him. Suddenly, however, a bulkhead door opened and Willett re-appeared.

'Put these on.'

He thrust a bundle of garments at the boy. Nat quickly pulled on a pair of white trousers and a blue Guernsey jumper. The trousers were too long and he had to roll them up at the ankles but at least he was warm.

Bosun Willett stood watching him, measuring and gauging, hardly bothering to conceal the dislike in his face. When Nat had finished dressing the old sailor beckoned him over.

'Right, boy,' he said. 'This is the Industrial School Ship *Havannah*. For your information – and I advise you to take note – she's a very historic vessel. She was one of the ships that escorted Napoleon into exile on St Helena, for a start. Then she sailed around the world – not once, but twice.'

He paused to glare at Nat.

'Know who Napoleon was, boy?'

Nat nodded. 'Yes. He was the French Emperor. He was defeated at the Battle of Waterloo in 1815.'

The Bosun pursed his lips and made a pretence of carefully studying his finger tips. When he spoke again his voice was low and measured but Nat instinctively understood the threat.

'All right, my friend, I'll tell you this once and once only. When you talk to me you say, "Sir". Is that clear?'

Again Nat nodded. He knew what he had to say.

'Yes. Sir.'

'Good. You'd be wise not to forget it. Now, then, the

14

Havannah. Despite the past, these days she's got a rather different role. For ten years she's been laid up here as a School Ship, an Industrial School Ship. Know what that means, Mr Smart?'

Nat shook his head. He saw Bosun Willett clench his fist and remembered just in time.

'No, sir.'

Willett smiled but there was little warmth in the expression. He moved closer and bent his head towards Nat. His breath smelled of tobacco smoke and rum and his fingers, Nat noticed, were knotted and scarred.

'As far as you're concerned, Industrial Schools only exist to control scum like you. Some Industrial Schools are run as farms, others like factories. Some – like the *Havannah* – are ships. The one common factor is the garbage they try to educate. It's a place of punishment, boy, where they send people who won't help themselves. You've been sent here because you were found begging in the streets. And so were the rest of the boys on board – all sixty-eight of them.'

He paused and gathered himself to his full height.

'We're going to control you, teach you a little discipline. But, more important, we're going to train you, instruct you in a profession that will be useful in your life. We're going to turn you into a sailor.'

'But I don't want to be a sailor,' Nat blurted out. 'I want . . .'

Bosun Willett punched him, hard, in the stomach. Nat doubled up in pain, wincing and desperately gasping for air. He felt the Bosun's calloused fingers in the back of his hair and his head was suddenly pulled upwards. Forcing back the tears, Nat heard Bosun Willett speaking softly but venomously into his ear.

15

'What you want doesn't count, scum. Only the law counts and the law has sent you here, to my tender mercies. You won't be a drain on society any more but you *will* become a sailor. And God help you if you don't learn quickly.'

Contemptuously, he thrust the boy away.

'In a minute we're going in to see the Superintendent, Mr Young. Listen to what he tells you but . . .' He hesitated, finger hovering beneath Nat's nose. 'Remember that I run this ship. Not Mr Bloody Young.'

The Bosun's arm jerked and his fist slammed into Nat's head. The boy reeled back against the bath tub, anger rising like a wave inside his belly. A deep hatred for this man had already begun to build and harden. Yet something inside his brain told Nat to keep his temper in check – for the time being.

'Yes, sir,' he mumbled.

Bosun Willett smiled grimly and nodded his head in satisfaction. He walked across the room and casually threw open the door.

'Follow me,' he said.

Chapter Two

JANUARY 1870

Following Bosun Willett's broad back down the passageway Nat's brain was working furiously. He had to get away. However hard life was on the streets of Newport, it certainly wasn't ever like this. Out there he was cold and alone but at least nobody told him what to do. As long as he stayed clear of the police and the other street gangs he could get by. Out there all the decisions were his.

Bosun Willett would beat him at the slightest provocation, of that he was quite sure. And the other adults would probably all be the same. He had to get away.

How to do it, that was the question. He could take to his heels now and run. The Bosun would never be able to keep up with him. He shrugged and shook his head – it was a foolish notion. He didn't know how to get out of this labyrinth of passageways and rooms; they would catch him long before he found his way off the ship and it would mean yet another beating.

Fine, he thought, for the moment I'm stuck here, I'll find a way out soon enough. He only knew that he had to get away, he just had to.

The Bosun came to a sudden halt before a thick oak door at the end of the passageway. Gathering himself, he smoothed down his hair and squared back his shoulders.

Yet Nat saw the contempt in his eyes. Whatever he felt about the Superintendent, it certainly wasn't respect.

'Remember what I said, boy,' Willett snarled suddenly, out of the corner of his mouth. 'Who runs this ship?'

'You do. Sir.'

The Bosun nodded grimly. 'Good.'

He knocked, lightly, on the door. There was no response. He knocked again, louder this time, and was rewarded by a muffled shout from within. Briskly, he turned the handle and pushed Nat ahead of him into the room.

Douglas Young sat behind a large mahogany desk. The cabin was spacious and Nat gazed at the wide window which ran behind the Superintendent's back, across the full width of the ship's stern. He could see the lights of Cardiff docks and rain, horizontal as stair rods, across the bay. Mr Young was rosy-cheeked and middle-aged. He wore a light blue suit and seemed happy to see him.

'Hello, young man,' he beamed. 'Welcome to the *Havannah*.'

Instinctively Nat recognised kindness in the man's voice. At the same time he felt, rather than saw, Bosun Willett's grimace of dislike from behind him. The Superintendent spoke quickly, telling him about the ship and what would happen to him.

'Work hard, learn quickly and you'll be all right,' he said at last. 'Our merchant navy always needs sailors and there are lots of openings here in this port – one of the greatest ports in Britain. That's why you were sent, you know, to learn a good, honest trade. We'll make a man of him yet, won't we, Emma?'

He glanced towards the far side of the cabin and for the first time Nat realised there was somebody else in room. A tall blonde girl, pretty and fresh, her hair bobbed and tied with ribbons, was sitting on a long couch, staring at him intently. Nat glanced towards her and thought he had never seen anyone so clean.

'Let me introduce you,' said Mr Young, coming out from behind his desk. 'This is Emma, my daughter. Emma should have been in bed hours ago but as soon as her Governess went off duty she decided to come here and keep me company. Emma, this is Nat Thomas. He's just arrived to join us.'

He smiled at her and it was clear, even then, that Douglas Young could refuse his daughter nothing. Emma leapt to her feet and came skipping across the carpet towards Nat. Stopping three feet short she put her head on one side and stared at him from under her fringe.

'How old are you?' she smiled.

'Eleven.'

'Say "Miss",' he heard the Bosun growl.

'Eleven, Miss; I think.'

'Don't you know?' Emma laughed. 'Fancy not knowing how old you are. I'm twelve. I'm very pleased to meet you, Nat Thomas.'

She held out her hand. Unsure, Nat took it gingerly. Her touch was warm and gentle. She laughed and bounced back to the couch. She picked up her book again but Nat knew that she was looking at him from under her fringe. Her interest pleased him but he could not really say why.

'No doubt you'll be seeing Emma around the ship,' Mr Young said. 'She lives here, with me, on board. Now then, young Nat, what do you think of the *Havannah*?'

Nat shrugged. Mr Young smiled.

'Oh, I don't suppose she looks much like a ship to you. All that housing on the top deck, for a start.'

'Makes it look like Noah's Ark,' called Emma from her couch.

Nat smiled to himself, strangely pleased that both he and Emma should have the same picture in their heads. Mr Young nodded, absent-mindedly.

'I suppose it does, really. But we had to do it, you see, Nat. To make classrooms and instruction areas so that you can train to be a sailor. Would you like to go to sea, Nat?'

Nat shrugged.

'Don't know.'

'I've told you before,' growled Bosun Willett, from somewhere behind him. 'Keep a civil tongue in your head when you talk to your betters.'

Nat saw Douglas Young's eyes swing towards the Bosun. Slowly he shook his head.

'Give him time, Bosun. This is all new to the boy.'

He patted Nat lightly on the shoulder and for some reason – something which the boy could not explain – Nat smiled up at him. He felt an unexpected warmth for this man. There was friendliness here and it felt good. Douglas Young ruffled his hair and went back to his desk.

'Run along with the Bosun, Nat. Do as he tells you.'

They went out, Nat following Bosun Willett along the dark passageway. Halfway down the corridor the Bosun paused in his stride and looked around. Then he reached to his left and threw open a hidden door in the corridor wall. He pushed Nat into a small cabin and pointed his finger.

'Stay here. And don't move. Understand?'

The door closed softly behind him and Nat was left alone. There was no furniture in the room, nowhere to sit and wait, so he leant against the bulkhead wall. Presently he slumped down onto the floor and tried, desperately, to think through the situation. So much had happened over the past few days, it was difficult to know where to begin.

Who did they think they were? Nobody had cared about him when his mother had died, so why did they bother now? If only his mother hadn't died. It had been fine before then. He couldn't remember what she looked like, his mother, but had built up a picture or an image of her in his mind.

He was never really able to see her clearly, her face and form always being blurred or misty at the edges. Yet there was always warmth and security surrounding her – a roaring fire in the background, food on the table, pictures on the wall. The image gave him comfort in the dark, cold nights.

They had sent him to live with a distant aunt in west Wales when she had died. It was awful. He had slept in an attic room and was always cold and hungry. His days were spent in the fields or barns of the farm, working from dawn until dusk. Even Sundays brought little relief. Then it was chapel three times, the rest of the day being spent on his knees reading the Bible or praying. His aunt and uncle had beaten him regularly; scourging out the wickedness they called it.

For six months he had endured it all and then, one day, he had simply run away. He had run and kept on running. It had taken him five days to get back to Newport. He had been living there, on the streets, ever since. It was a hard existence but at least it was familiar. The only real problems had been how to survive the day or night. Until now. Now he was here, on the *Havannah*, and he had to get away.

'If they think I'm staying,' Nat hissed suddenly to the empty room, 'then they must think I'm bloody stupid.'

He stood up and crossed to the porthole. It was still raining. He tried to turn the retaining screw on the port but it had been painted over many times and simply refused to move. All right, it would have to be the door.

He padded across to the entrance and listened carefully. There was no sound from outside. Slowly he turned the handle and peered out. There was no sign of Bosun Willett. To the right lay Douglas Young's office – there was no escape that way. Nat turned left.

Silently, he eased down the passageway. From around the corner at the far end came a dim gleam of light and, as he came closer, he was able to pick out the low rumble of voices.

'Damn!' he swore and started to creep back the way he had come.

Then he heard the Bosun's voice. For some reason he was never able to understand Nat knew he had to hear what was being said. He flattened himself against the wall and inched forward. The voices were louder now. Around the corner the passage opened out into a small hall or stair-well and there, illuminated by the glow of a bulkhead oil lamp, stood Bosun Willett and the dark-suited man who had brought him here an hour before.

'It's all you're getting, damn you!' the dark-suited man snarled suddenly. 'There's overheads, you know. I can't afford any more.'

The Bosun raised his hand.

'Keep your voice down, you fool! Your overheads are your problem. I'm the one who takes the risks – if the bloody Superintendent or anybody from the Committee should start asking questions, they won't be asking them of you. I keep the brats on short rations, I do all the dirty work. If you want the goods then you can buy them at my price. Otherwise there's plenty of people in the market who'll be happy to take them at whatever price I care to charge.'

Nat's gaze flickered to three bulging sacks which lay at the foot of the stairs. Even as he watched the two men swung around to stare at the sacks. Finally Bosun Willett shrugged.

'Well, you know what's there, Mr Best. Beef joints, biscuits, flour, even a couple of dozen pairs of trousers. You'll be making yourself a small fortune. And there'll be more next week – that's the key, the bonus, so to speak. Every week you'll get the same. Or more. Take it or leave it, Mr Best. I'm a busy man.'

Mr Best, as the Bosun called him, licked his lips and smiled. His anger had gone, only greed remained. Feigning reluctance, he reached into his jacket pocket and counted out a sheaf of white five-pound notes.

'You're robbing me something rotten, Bosun,' he smiled, handing over the notes. 'I don't know how I'm going to make anything out of this deal, anything at all.'

Bosun Willett did not answer. He pushed across the sacks and watched as Mr Best shouldered them and inclined his head in farewell. Slowly he climbed up the companionway stairs and disappeared from view. For several seconds Bosun Willett remained staring after him.

Suddenly and without warning, the Bosun swung around and marched purposefully towards the passageway. Nat looked around – with horror he realised that there was nowhere to hide and not enough time to run. He felt his stomach churn and then the Bosun was suddenly on him.

'What the devil are you doing here?' Bosun Willett roared, grabbing Nat by the jersey and pulling him close. 'What did you see? Come on, what did you see?'

'Nothing,' Nat gasped. 'I've only just got here. You were so long I thought you'd forgotten me.'

Bosun Willett glared at him and his fingers tightened their grip. Almost without emotion, Nat realised that he was being lifted off the floor. Slowly, but with increasing violence, he felt himself shaken, back and forth, like a child's rag doll.

'What did you see? Tell me?'

The Bosun's face had grown very red. Nat felt his teeth bang together and his head swam. It was becoming increasingly hard to breathe.

'Nothing,' he managed to blurt out, fingers clawing desperately at the Bosun's hands. 'Nothing. Honest. I didn't see a thing.'

Reluctantly, Willett stopped shaking him. Nat's feet touched the deck again but the man still held him in a grip as strong as iron.

'For your sake, boy, I hope you didn't. But if, by any chance you did see something, then a word of warning. Forget it. Now, right now. Forget it. Understand?'

Nat nodded, swallowing hard. He did not know the significance of what he had seen but it obviously meant something to the Bosun. That was fine. He would store the memory and use it when the time was right.

'Remember what I say – or you'll regret it. Now it's late. Time you were put out of harm's way.'

Snarling, the Bosun dragged him along the passageway and down to the lower deck. They went into a long, dark dormitory where canvas shapes, like white shrouds or rolled up sails, stretched the length and breadth of the room. There was barely a sound, apart from a low and regular humming – breathing, Nat realised, many men or boys breathing.

'That's your berth,' growled Willett, pointing to one of the shapes. 'Get in and get to sleep.'

Nat had never slept in a hammock. He put his arms on the canvas and swung himself up. The bed shot from under him and he somersaulted onto the cold deck. The room exploded into laughter.

'Quiet, you bastards!' roared Willett.

He seized Nat by the scruff of the neck and hauled him to his feet. Viciously, he pulled him close.

'Listen! Don't try to be funny with me, boy. Get into that hammock, now.'

'But I can't. I don't know how.'

Another burst of laughter echoed around the room, instantly stilled by Willett's withering glare. The Bosun shook his head in disbelief. Reaching out, he held the canvas rigid.

'Now try.'

With difficulty, Nat climbed into the hammock, pulled the blanket up to his chin and lay quietly.

'Not a sound,' hissed Willett to the silent room.

Nat lay in the hammock for what seemed like hours. Outside, the rain beat heavily against the wooden hull of the *Havannah*. Nobody spoke or moved but he knew that unseen eyes were watching him. And he felt the fear.

Chapter Three

JANUARY TO FEBRUARY 1870

It seemed as if he had just closed his eyes when the shrill blast of a whistle brought Nat bolt upright in the hammock. The canvas bed swung alarmingly beneath him and he tumbled in a heap onto the floor.

'That's one way of getting up in the morning.'

A ginger-haired boy in the hammock alongside him was laughing and nodding his head.

Nat stared at him. The boy's hair stood nearly upright on the top of his head and his freckled face was creased in a broad smile. Despite himself, Nat laughed too.

'Tommy Jenkins,' announced the strange boy, vaulting with amazing agility out of his hammock. 'From Pembroke Dock, down west. Who are you?'

'Nat Thomas. From Newport.'

'Pleased to meet you, Nat. Come on, we can be first in the queue for washing if we're quick.'

He pulled Nat to his feet and led the way to an open space at the rear of the dormitory. It had stopped raining, Nat noticed, but it was still pitch black outside. A row of metal basins stood on wooden racks. Tommy poured ice cold water into one of the basins and thrust in his head.

'Come on. Be quick or the Bosun'll be round with a length of rope across your back.'

Nat copied his new friend and towelled himself dry on a piece of canvas sacking. By now the other boys had begun to appear. All over the ship officers' whistles were being blown in an unlikely but effective dawn chorus.

A mop and bucket were thrust into Nat's hands and, in company with Tommy Jenkins and several others, he spent an hour scrubbing the dormitory deck. Officers patrolled the room, making sure the work was carried out. All of them, Nat noticed, carried a short piece of rope, knotted at the end. None of them seemed too unhappy about using these weapons on the back of anybody who was slow or slacking at his job.

'Soon be breakfast,' breathed Tommy as they finally stored away their buckets. 'Hungry?'

Nat nodded. He hadn't eaten for over twenty-four hours and he suddenly realised there were sharp pangs of hunger in his stomach. Daylight had broken while they worked and Nat knew that he needed to eat, to keep up his strength. The new day meant new opportunities to escape.

Breakfast, when it came, consisted of porridge and two large wedges of bread.

'Porridge again,' complained Tommy. 'We're supposed to get kippers every other day. It's always bloody porridge.'

Nat couldn't have cared less. The meal was hot and filling. He drank two cups of tea, without milk or sugar, and wiped his bowl clean with the remains of his bread. They could give him porridge every meal, every day of the week, for all he cared.

'So how do you like the *Havannah*?' asked Tommy as they sat waiting for orders.

Nat shrugged.

'I don't know. I'm not staying, so it doesn't matter.'

Tommy and the boys alongside him exploded into laughter. Nat felt the colour rush to his face and leapt to his feet, fists clenched. Quickly Tommy pulled him back down onto the bench.

'Don't be stupid. We're only having a bit of fun. No fighting on deck – it's a rule. You get the birch for breaking rules.'

Nat's temper subsided and he relaxed .

'So you're not stopping, eh?'

'That's right. I'm going to escape, first chance I get. You'll see.'

Tommy shrugged. His shock of ginger hair, vertical on top of his head, wagged as he talked Nothing, it seemed, could ever make the hair lie flat to his scalp.

'So just how are you going to escape, eh? Jump off the top deck? It's fifty feet down to the water – or to the mud, most of the time. And that's six feet deep. So you'll break your neck or drown or maybe suffocate – whichever way, you'll be dead. Which, I suppose, is escaping in a way. It's your choice, kid.'

Nat frowned at him. What Tommy said seemed to make sense.

'There's got to be other ways?'

'Really? If there are then I'd like to know about them. Nobody ever goes off the ship without half a dozen turnkeys to keep them company.'

'What's a turnkey?'

Tommy shook his head.

'God, you have got a lot to learn, aint you? Turnkey – a guard or a warder. Not that this lot are real warders. They're Instructors, though *they* like to call themselves

Officers. But it's no difference, they all do the same job. They're here to make sure *you* stay here. And then there's Bosun Willett. But you've already met him, haven't you?'

Nat nodded. He had heard the Bosun's voice already that morning, bellowing at somebody on the upper deck. As yet, however, he had not caught sight of the man. That suited Nat perfectly. He would be happy if he never saw him again. For several minutes there was silence, everybody thinking of the day ahead. Suddenly, Tommy nudged him in the ribs.

'They're coming in with the Orders of the Day. Stick close to me – that way you'll probably end up in my Watch.'

Nat stared at him, eyebrows raised, not really understanding what the boy was talking about. Tommy was about the same age as Nat but he seemed to have a knowing and practical edge to him. He certainly seemed to understand the ropes on board the *Havannah*. It would be as well to learn from him, Nat decided.

'They'll divide us into two Watches,' Tommy explained, quickly, 'two groups. Port and Starboard. One Watch goes into the schoolroom with Mr Young, the other does nautical training with the Bosun. After a couple of hours the Watches change round. It's all quite simple; you'll soon pick it up.'

Tommy Jenkins was quite right. When his turn came, Nat found himself allocated to the Port Watch along with his new friend. Under the careful gaze of two Officers they were ushered into the classroom on the upper deck. Douglas Young stood at the far end of the room.

'Good morning, boys,' he called, beaming at them. 'Take your seats quickly.'

The lessons were simple enough – English, reading and arithmetic. Yet most of the boys had never been near a schoolroom and Douglas Young was hard pushed to give them the time they needed. He was pleasantly surprised when it came to Nat's turn to read.

'Well done, young man. A little rusty, perhaps, but you've certainly got the basics. Who taught you?'

'My mother, sir. Then an aunt, after my mother died. I . . . I just haven't had much call for reading over the past few years.'

Mr Young nodded and patted him on the shoulder.

'Indeed not! Indeed not. Well, now's your chance to make up for lost time. Work hard and in a week or so we'll have you reading Charles Dickens.'

Nat glowed with unexpected pleasure. He was amazed at how much he enjoyed the school work and bent over his slate with a will. All too soon, however, the Watches changed and it was their turn for Bosun Janye's tender care.

If Douglas Young had taught with kindness, the Bosun believed in the use of fear and raw power to instruct the boys. The task, that first day, was learning to scull *Havannah*'s longboat. The Watch obediently followed Bosun Willett to a landing stage alongside the old ship. As they came down the gangway and headed off towards the river Nat glanced urgently around – surely this was his chance?

Two other Officers walked at the back of the column, however, and the path between the ship and landing stage was narrow. He would be lucky to make ten yards, he decided. He would have to wait a while longer, yet.

Moored alongside the landing stage was a heavy wooden rowing boat. It must have been thirty feet long, Nat thought, and now it lay, rocking gently in the swell of the river. Gingerly he followed Tommy and took his place in the boat.

'You idle bloody ruffians,' the Bosun cursed. 'Bend your backs.'

He stood in the stern sheets, waving his knotted rope, as the boys of the Port Watch sweated and strained at the heavy oars. Three times the rope came down on the heads of unlucky boys. Nat was glad that he was in the bow of the boat, well away from the Bosun's wrath.

Manoeuvring the long boat away from the jetty was not an easy task, as Tommy informed Nat in breathless gasps. It was far too easy to miss your stroke or simply strike the mud of the river bed instead of the water.

Soon, however, the boat was out in the stream and the boys lapsed into an easy rhythm at their oars. Bosun Willett sat in the stern, rocking the tiller, and the longboat moved easily past the rows of moored ships. There was a feeling of calm contentment and the air was fresh after the previous night's rain.

Even Bosun Willett seemed lulled into a quiet ease. He pulled out his pipe, puffing happily as the boys worked. Soon he was pointing out landmarks and ships as they passed them by.

'What's that one called, sir?' asked one of the older boys as they swept alongside a huge, three-masted sailing ship which was anchored in the centre of the Bay.

Tommy Jenkins nudged Nat in the ribs and inclined his head towards the boy who had just spoken.

31

'Jimmy Baker. A right bloody toady, well in the Bosun's pocket. Watch out for him.'

'No talking down there!' bellowed the Bosun.

Tommy and Nat bent to their oars and Bosun Willett gazed at the ship on their starboard quarter.

'That, boy, is the *Le Hogue*. She's what we call a Blackwell Frigate. Unusual vessel. The poop deck runs to her main mast, nearly 100 feet long. See, boy? Owned by Devitt and Moore.'

Out into the Bay they sculled. The water here was choppier but the Bosun seemed not to notice.

'Penarth Head,' he called, pointing with the stem of his pipe. 'Remember it and the church steeple – St Augustine's, it's called. Best landmark you'll ever see, beating up the Channel. Stands out for miles.'

They were almost round Penarth Head now and a heavy sea was running. Several times the bow of the longboat bit into large waves as spray and seawater slopped in over the side. Just short of the Bristol Channel, however, Bosun Willett turned the boat around and, with the tide behind them, they swept back towards the *Havannah*. Despite being wet to the skin, Nat was disappointed. He had thoroughly enjoyed the outing.

And so the days began to fall into a regular pattern. Tommy had been right. There was little – if any – opportunity to escape. Each day, from dawn until dusk, was taken up with school lessons and instruction in seamanship. At lights-out Nat was usually too tired to do anything but fall into his hammock, with escape the last thing on his mind.

In lessons, under the gentle direction of Douglas Young, Nat grew in confidence and skill. All the letters and words his mother had taught him so many years ago quickly came back to him and, soon, he found himself in the top form of the school.

Despite Bosun Willett's methods of teaching he also grew to enjoy the nautical training. It was basic instruction – tying knots, rowing boats, learning how to steer – but it was all new and enthralling to Nat. The *Havannah* was a grounded hulk, moored and anchored to the bank of the River Taff. She might once have been a great ship but now she was wedged firmly on the mud and would never sail again.

Nat had always had a fertile imagination. Thanks to Mr Young's urging and encouragement his creativity flourished once again – now, in his mind, the *Havannah* became, once more, a mighty ship of war, ploughing through mountainous seas, defending Britain's trade routes. He tried to explain his feelings to Tommy and the others one evening but was met only by bland expressions and incredulity. Several of the boys sniggered.

'Are you stupid of something?' responded one tall lad by the name of Morgan Spencer. 'It's a bloody prison, that's all!'

Tommy Jenkins glared at the boys and they subsided into silence. Gently he took Nat's arm and pulled him away.

'They don't understand, Nat,' he said. 'Blowed if I do myself, come to that. I think it's just that clever dammed brain of yours playing tricks. Imagination, it's called. And that's a dangerous thing for people like you and me.'

He patted Nat, lightly, on the arm and wandered away to the other side of the room. Nat shook his head. Tommy was right – they didn't understand, any of

33

them. Almost without knowing it, the old ship had begun to mean something quite special to him. Yet it was a feeling, an emotion, that only he seemed to have.

Lessons in seamanship usually took place on the upper deck or in the longboat. Despite his slight build Nat was wiry and strong and he loved nothing better than to pull at the big oars which sent the longboat winging up and down river. He was good at the job but he knew that others hated him for his skill.

'Just look at that creep,' sneered Jimmy Baker as they pulled back up the river one day. 'Always trying to impress the Bosun.'

Nat glanced across at the boy. Jimmy was a big, ungainly lout, two or three years older than Tommy and himself, and he seemed to have taken an instant dislike to him. Rarely a day went by without Jimmy making some remark or pushing him out of the way in the queue for food. Nat shrugged and kept his thoughts to himself – there would have to be a reckoning, he knew, but not just yet.

Once or twice during his first month he saw Emma Young, walking down a passageway or taking the air on the upper deck. She was usually with Miss Clarkson, her Governess. The venerable lady was tall, with a hooked nose, and was usually clad in black. An air of gloom seemed to accompany her, wherever she went. Her dark bonnet and shawl contrasted sharply with Emma's whites and pinks. Like all the other boys on the *Havannah*, Nat thought Emma looked like an angel.

Each time they passed each other Emma would smile but she never spoke. Nat, unaccountably, could not help wishing she would talk to him again. 'She's probably forgotten who I am,' he told himself and sadly went on to other jobs. Then, one Sunday, as the boys were marching to the mess hall after the morning church service, Emma came skipping along the passageway towards them. Miss Clarkson trailed, breathlessly, ten yards behind. To Nat's surprise Emma came to a halt alongside him.

'My father wants to see you,' she announced. 'Now. In his cabin.'

She looked up as Bosun Willett came towards them and repeated her message. The Bosun frowned and, for a brief second, a spasm of alarm flickered across his face. He glanced at Miss Clarkson who had now managed to catch up with her charge.

'She's quite right,' said the Governess, sniffing, 'Mr Young wishes to see the boy now.'

'Ten minutes,' Willett growled. 'No more. I put him in your charge, Miss.'

He stared at a point somewhere between Emma and Miss Clarkson and it was impossible to know exactly whom he was addressing.

It was the first time since he had come to the *Havannah* that Nat was out of the direct sight of one of the Officers. Yet, strangely, the thought of running away, of seizing his chance and going over the side, never entered his head. He meekly followed Emma towards Douglas Young's office at the stern of the ship. Once again, Miss Clarkson was soon left, panting, behind.

'How are you getting on?' Emma asked, over her shoulder.

'Good,' he responded. 'It's nice to be warm and well fed.'

'Well fed? I don't know how you boys live on what they give you.'

35

'It's better than what I'm used to.'

Emma glanced back at him from under arched eyebrows.

'My father says you're very clever. He says you can read better than many adults.'

'My mother taught me. We used to spend hours just reading and talking. I used to love her books. She had hundreds of them, all around her room. They were all sold when she died.'

For a moment Emma was silent. Then she reached out and put her hand on his arm, bringing Nat to a sudden halt.

'Father has lots of books. Dickens, Thackeray, people I've never even heard of. I'm sure he'd let you read them.'

They walked on and Emma led the way into the cabin. Douglas Young was standing with his back to the door, staring out of the wide stern window. He spun around when they entered and smiled at them.

'Ah, young Nat. Just the man. Sit down, sit down.'

Warily Nat perched himself on the edge of a chair. He was not used to such pleasantries and half expected Bosun Willett to appear, screaming and punching, from behind the desk or door.

'Now then,' said Mr Young, sitting opposite him, 'I have been very impressed by your progress in class, Nat. You've done well. But I can't give you all the time you need, all the attention you deserve. Others have more pressing problems – I don't need to go on; you know what I mean.'

He paused and stared around the cabin. Slowly he nodded his head.

'You have real ability, Nat. I don't think I've ever

36

seen more promise in a boy – certainly not in any boy on the *Havannah*. So I am about to make you an offer.'

Again he paused. Suddenly he reached across and held out a glass dish of sugared almonds. Warily, Nat stared at the Superintendent but the man just nodded and pushed the dish closer to him. Carefully, delicately, Nat took an almond and put it in his mouth.

'Good?'

Nat nodded, enjoying the unusual taste on his tongue. His mouth was filled with saliva and he could not speak. Douglas Young tapped him on the knee.

'Nat? If you would care to come here, say three or four evenings a week – after your day's work is finished – then I will teach you. I coach Emma in the evenings – she needs someone to measure herself against, to compete with. Together you will both learn quicker and I can give you more time. What do you say?'

Nat was still wary. Why should anybody care enough about him to make such an offer? What did this man want? What was in it for him? As if she could sense his thoughts, Emma suddenly spoke.

'It's all right, Nat. Father hates to see wasted talent. He can see a talent in you; he just wants you to use your ability – and it will help me. Please say yes.'

'But what about Bosun Willett?'

Douglas Young shook his head.

'Don't worry about the Bosun. I'll arrange everything with him. The offer is there, Nat, if you want to take it.'

Nat stared at them, Emma and her father. Such kindness astounded him. He could have cried. Slowly he nodded his head.

'Yes. Please.'

Douglas Young took him back to the mess deck. The boys were already seated, waiting for the cooks to bring in their food. Nat slipped into his seat alongside Tommy Jenkins and Morgan Spencer. The ginger-haired boy stared at him, eyes alive with questions.

'What was that about?' he hissed from the corner of his mouth.

'I'll tell you later,' Nat whispered.

He stared across to the front of the room, to where Douglas Young and Bosun Willett were standing. Their conversation was animated and Mr Young, quiet and gentle as he was, seemed to be making his point strongly.

Even as Nat looked, Bosun Willett glanced urgently towards him. The hatred and fear were alive and burning in his eyes.

Chapter Four

FEBRUARY TO APRIL 1870

Over the next few months Nat worked hard at his lessons. Three or four evenings each week, after the day's instruction was over, he was escorted to the Superintendent's cabin and there, with Emma, he spent several hours poring over books and papers.

Most of the other boys found it difficult to understand why he wanted to do it.

'I'd rather sleep,' shrugged Morgan Spencer. 'Lessons is hard enough in the day, why bother doing extra?'

Only Tommy seemed to understand.

'Just leave him alone,' he said, putting a protective arm around Nat's shoulders. 'He's got more brains in his little finger that you've got in your whole body. What's wrong with trying to improve yourself? Going to be a ship's captain, is our Nat.'

Jimmy Baker and his cronies kept up a constant stream of abuse. As far as they were concerned Nat was only sucking up to the Superintendent and that gave them the chance they needed to poke fun and bully.

It did not take long for Jimmy Baker's dislike to flare into open hostility. One night, the boys were herded into a room low on the ship's waterline. Converted into a playroom, it was now equipped with draughts, cards, papers and magazines.

'This is Mr Young's idea,' explained Tommy. 'He set it up last year. Trouble is, we only get to use it now and again. More's the pity.'

Nat frowned.

'But why? If it was his idea, surely he'd be pleased to see us using it more often?'

Tommy sneered and threw himself into a seat.

'Oh, *he* would, sure. But he's weak. Come on, Nat, you know that. Bosun Willett runs this ship and you've seen what he's like. I think you going to him for extra lessons is the only thing Mr Young's ever insisted on.'

Despite himself, Nat knew that his friend was right. Douglas Young had the power to make their lives so much better and, yet, for some reason he seemed to allow Bosun Willett to run the *Havannah* as he chose. And the way the Bosun chose was with a kick rather than kindness, with a sneer rather than a soft word.

'If we're lucky, we get to come down here once every couple of months. Bosun Willett hates us doing anything but work.'

Tommy pulled a pack of playing cards and a cribbage board from one of the drawers in the table. He held them out to Nat.

'Want a game?'

'I don't know how.'

'With your head,' Tommy laughed, 'you'll pick it up soon enough. Sit down and I'll teach you.'

For a brief hour under the watchful but resentful gaze of the old sailor, the boys played and read. Nat soon picked up the game and its scoring system. He was happily playing when, suddenly, he felt a heavy hand on his shoulder.

'Shove off, kid, I want to play.'

40

It was Jimmy Baker, looming over him and grinning. Nat glanced across to the side of the room but Bosun Willett had turned his back and seemed to be intently studying something on the bulkhead.

'Move, I said.'

Nat shook his head, anger and resentment beginning to build, deep inside his chest.

'I'm playing.'

The bigger boy reached down and grabbed Nat's jumper, yanking him painfully to his feet. Instinctively, almost before he knew what he was doing, Nat lashed out. Jimmy might have been bigger and older but years of living rough on the streets of Newport had honed Nat's reactions to a fine art.

'Never fight,' one of the older street boys had told him, many years before, 'unless you want to kill him or put him in hospital.'

It was good advice. Nat's fist caught Jimmy flush on the point of his nose and the bigger boy fell back, blood spurting through clenched fingers.

'Ow! You bastard! You've broken my bloody nose.'

All the instincts of the street came rushing back into Nat's brain.

'When you've got your enemy down,' his old comrade of the back alleys had said, 'don't ease off. That's when you go in and finish him.'

Nat gritted his teeth and lunged forward. His second blow caught Jimmy on the top of his head. The boy howled in pain and cowered backwards. Nat gathered himself for the final strike but, suddenly, strong arms encircled him. He struggled but was unable to move.

'Fighting on deck, eh?' Bosun Willett hissed into his ear. 'It's the brig for you, my boy.'

Nat knew he had nothing to lose. He kicked backwards with his heel and felt a satisfying crunch as he made contact with the Bosun's shin. His pleasure did not last long. The Bosun cursed and hurled him across the room. He cannoned into a table and crashed heavily to the deck. Before he had time to move Bosun Willett's boot slammed into his ribs.

'Little bastard!'

Gasping for breath, Nat looked up and saw the Bosun rubbing his leg. He tried to climb to his feet but another vicious kick sent him sprawling once more.

'You'll get the birch for this, Nat Thomas!'

The Bosun was right. Two Officers dragged Nat to a small cell at the bow of the ship – the brig, as it was commonly known. He spent the night there, shivering with the cold. There was no bed and he had no blankets. His ribs hurt where the Bosun had kicked him but he knew that he would receive no medical help.

All night long he lay on the cold floor and seethed with righteous anger. Damn Jimmy and damn the Bosun, too. It was their fault that he was here. And yet it was no more than he had expected. Trust people, try to make something of your life, and in the end you'll just get kicked in the teeth. He should have known better.

Early the following morning he was marched in before the Superintendent and made to stand at attention in front of the desk. Emma, he noticed, was nowhere in sight.

'Why, Nat?' Douglas Young asked, reproachfully. 'Why did you do it? Why did you attack the Bosun?'

Nat shrugged and made no answer. It did not matter, they were going to punish him, whatever he said. And at least he had got in one good kick at the Bosun. Mr

Young questioned him for some time but he just shook his head and refused to speak. In the end he was sentenced to six strokes of the birch, the punishment to be inflicted by Bosun Willett in front of the entire ship's company.

He was led back to his cell to await punishment. For two or three hours he lay on the cold deck and waited. Then, at last, he heard the sharp blasts of Officers' whistles summoning the boys onto the upper deck. The muffled thud of their running feet on the boards above his head told him that they were almost ready for him. The cell door suddenly crashed open and Jimmy Baker and the Bosun stood before him.

'It's time,' growled Willett.

Jimmy grinned at him.

'Let's see how you enjoy this,' he hissed as Nat was led up the companionway.

A six-foot plank had been tied to one of the beams – the whipping post. Nat shuddered and tried to push down his fear.

'This'll teach you to hit me,' whispered Jimmy.

The boy's voice was thick and nasal. Clearly he was having trouble breathing through his damaged nose. As the Bosun's assistant, Jimmy had an important role to play. Before Nat was lashed to the post he gleefully stripped off the smaller boy's jersey and then stood grinning as the Bosun flexed his muscles.

'Enjoy it,' he said. 'I know I will.'

Nat stared at him, speechless with hatred and fear.

'Begin,' called Mr Young.

Scared as he was, Nat was still able to see that Douglas Young was pale. His eyes kept darting towards Nat, then away towards the assembled ship's company.

He hates this, Nat realised, hates every minute of it. But he's got no choice.

The birching was bad, Bosun Willett using every ounce of his strength to inflict serious damage. Each stroke of the cane, a thin split bamboo rod, sliced into the flesh of Nat's back. He had determined not to cry out, to deprive Willett of the pleasure of making him weep, but on the fourth stroke a strangled groan escaped his lips. His back burned as if it had been set alight.

Afterwards, they took him down to the Sick Bay and Mr Taylor, the First Aid Instructor, dressed his wounds. The ointment stung, biting down into the open cuts. Nat felt tears in his eyes but he bit his lip and tried not to cry out, knowing that the pain was necessary.

'Keep still, boy,' growled the Officer. 'I can't do anything if you keep squirming around.'

Once, Nat glanced up and saw Douglas Young in the open doorway. The Superintendent stared at him and their eyes met. Slowly, almost imperceptibly, Young raised his eyebrows and then turned away.

That night, as he lay in his hammock, each swing or move of the *Havannah* causing his back to flare up once more, he knew that the attention of all the boys was on him. Nobody spoke to him, however, and even Bosun Willett found it hard to look him in the eye.

'Does it hurt?' asked Tommy Jenkins at breakfast the next day.

Nat shook his head, knowing that Tommy did not believe him but knowing, also, that the lie was both needed and expected. The boy who served out the porridge slipped him an extra large helping and winked at him. Clearly he had gone up in the boys' estimation.

In class, Mr Young was as pleasant as ever. At midmorning break, as the Watches changed over, Emma came dancing across to him.

'My father says, "Tonight, as usual". Is that all right, Nat?'

He nodded, embarrassed and ashamed to look her in the eye. She smiled at him and he knew that everything was back to normal. It was as if nothing had ever happened. Nat was relieved. He did not want to upset the Superintendent or his daughter.

Only Jimmy Baker spoiled things. At dinner time he sidled up to within three feet and stared coldly at Nat. Hatred burned in his watery blue eyes.

'Just you wait,' he snarled. 'You haven't even started to pay.'

And yet, Nat noticed, he kept that safe three feet away. Perhaps the boy had learned something after all.

That evening he worked particularly hard at his lessons. The time seemed to fly past and Nat was surprised when Douglas Young finally called a halt.

'That's enough for tonight,' he said. 'You and Emma sit there and watch the ships in the bay. I'll make us all a cup of cocoa.'

Nat sat with Emma on the wide bench beneath the stern window. The light had almost gone but the spars and rigging of hundreds of moored ships stood out starkly against the evening sky. Bright yellow lights glowed at each mast head and the rumble of sailors' laughter echoed from one of the nearer vessels.

Behind them, in the cabin, Emma's Governess, Miss Clarkson, dozed over her needlework. A low snore suddenly rolled across the room and Miss Clarkson jerked awake. Emma and Nat looked at each other and giggled.

'Does it hurt?' Emma asked, quietly.

Nat shrugged. 'Sometimes. When I move quickly.'

'What was it about, Nat? I know you wouldn't attack the Bosun without being provoked.'

He told her, quietly, about Jimmy and the incident in the Games Room. Emma listened, slowly shaking her head in disbelief.

'Why didn't you tell my father? He'd never have let Jimmy get away with it. Or the Bosun. Oh, I hate that man. Do you really think he set Jimmy up to it?'

Nat considered the question. As far as he could see there was no other explanation. Over the past few weeks Willett had become increasingly harsh in his dealings with Nat. He knew that if he was slow to an order or task, then the Bosun's boot or fist would lash out at him. His treatment was not too different from that of the other boys – Bosun Willett was notoriously hard and uncaring with his punishments. It was just that there was always an extra edge to his dealings with Nat, an extra viciousness to his kicks or punches. The boy could not explain it but he knew, only too well, that the threat to his safety was a very real one. He explained his feelings, now, to Emma.

'I think it got worse once I started to come here for lessons. It's as if he doesn't want me to succeed or get on.'

Emma smiled at him, reached across and squeezed his hand.

'Then you'll just have to try even harder, won't you? Just to get back at the old goat.'

Nat grinned. She was right – it was the only way to get even with the Bosun.

Chapter Five

MAY 1870

Early in May a tense excitement began to grip and run through the *Havannah*. It was hard for the boys to say exactly what it was all about, to identify the cause, but everybody sensed the tension. Officers were brisk about their tasks and even Bosun Willett appeared on duty with his beard neatly trimmed and combed.

'What the hell's going on?' Tommy Jenkins queried. 'You know old Trotty Taylor, the First Aid Instructor? He even offered to wash my arm when I cut it on the boat deck yesterday.'

'You must have been in a bad way,' commented Morgan Spencer. 'Bleedin' a lot, were you?'

Tommy shook his head.

'Nah. It was just a scratch. I don't know what's got into any of them. They're all being as nice as pie suddenly.'

'I reckon they've all gone barmy,' said Morgan. 'Like you hear about sailors on ships when they're becalmed. They'll probably start killing themselves soon. Or us!'

He leered at the other boys and everybody dissolved into laughter. The following morning, however, there was utter amazement when, at breakfast, a new and unusual aroma filled the air.

'What's that smell?' asked Nat.

Tommy paused and thrust his nose in the air. Delicately he sniffed. A grin began to steal across his face.

'I'll tell you what that is, boy. That's kippers, that's what that is. That's kippers!'

It was, Morgan Spencer later said, like Christmas and Easter rolled into one. For nearly fifteen glorious minutes the assembled ship's company spoke not a word but fought silently and devoutly to get their unexpected treat eaten and then – joy of all joys – to stand eagerly in the queue for seconds.

'Oh mother,' sighed Tommy, rolling his eyes to the heavens. 'I can die happily after this!'

It was Nat who discovered the cause of all their pleasure. That evening, when Douglas Young had finished his lesson and was making their usual cup of cocoa, as Miss Clarkson slept over her needlework, he told Emma about all the changes. She widened her eyes when she heard about Bosun Willett's beard and gravely nodded her head.

'It must be the inspection. Can't be anything else. The Bosun's trying to be nice so he'll be given a good report. Tell Nat about the inspection, Daddy.'

Douglas Young looked up from the hob where he was brewing the cocoa. He considered the request, then shrugged.

'There's no harm in Nat knowing. Nor any of the boys, for that matter.'

Carefully, he carried across three mugs of steaming cocoa and placed them on the desk.

'It's just the Home Office, Nat; the government, if you like. They give us a licence to run the *Havannah*. Every year they inspect us, to make sure that we are treating you correctly, educating you as well as you should be educated. The Rev Sydney Turner – he's the Chief Inspector – is coming here next Friday. He'll spend the day on board and then make a report on the state of the ship, the educational levels, on everything really.'

When Tommy Jenkins heard the news later that night, he whistled and nodded knowingly.

'Of course. Why else would we get kippers for breakfast?'

'Bloody Bosun Willett,' snarled Morgan. 'We ought to play up, be right bloody nuisances. That would get him a bad report, wouldn't it?'

Nat shook his head.

'No, Morgan. He'd only take it out on us later, when the Inspector's gone. I say let's enjoy the food and the good treatment while we can.'

Tommy and the others sagely nodded their heads. Nat's advice was sensible and well worth taking. Kippers for breakfast and plenty of meat for dinner – it wouldn't last but they should enjoy it while it did!

On the Thursday before the inspection Douglas Young unexpectedly appeared in the Mess Hall at dinner time. The boys nudged each other and stared. Mr Young never came to the Mess Hall, always leaving mealtime supervision to Bosun Willett and the other Officers.

'Wonder what he wants?' whispered Tommy.

The answer was not long in coming. Mr Young stared around the room and, when his eyes came to rest on Nat, he smiled and beckoned him over. Tommy frowned but Nat quickly got to his feet and trotted over to where Douglas Young and Bosun Willett stood at the front of the room.

'Remember, Mr Young,' the Bosun was saying, 'it's against my advice. I want that put on record. You can't trust these boys. None of 'em.'

49

'Call it an experiment, Bosun,' Douglas Young returned, 'if that makes you happier. I trust the boy. If he lets me down, then it's on my own head.'

He turned to Nat and stared at him gravely. Yet there was a twinkle deep within his eye.

'Nat, I need you to run an errand for me. There's a stall in the market which sells ledgers. You know those big, leather books that I write in? I need two of them now, before the inspection, and I want you to run along and get them for me.'

Nat was stunned. He stared at Mr Young. This meant going off the ship – and, more importantly, going off the ship unsupervised. It had never been known before. No wonder Bosun Willett was indignant.

'Can you do it, Nat?'

Hardly able to speak, Nat nodded his head. Douglas Young pressed a gold sovereign into his palm and led him out of the Mess Hall. The boys stared in wonder. Nat smiled at Tommy and shrugged his shoulders. From the corner of his eye he caught the look of thunderous anger on Bosun Willett's face and some of his pleasure immediately disappeared. Some but not all.

'I'll expect you back in two hours, Nat,' called Douglas Young from the top of the gangway.

Nat raced away, down the plank, overjoyed to be out in the fresh air. His stomach felt huge and he realised that it was pleasure, pleasure at being trusted and treated as a human being for once in his life.

'I'll be back in one, sir!' he shouted.

In the event, it took Nat longer than he had expected. It was a long walk to the centre of Cardiff and the pavements were thronged with pedestrians. For as far as the eye could see the streets were full of hackney cabs and top hats, of bright parasols and hurrying figures.

Nat clutched the sovereign tightly and gazed around. It would have been so easy to slip away, to run to the railway station and purchase a ticket. He could be in Newport again within thirty minutes. He thought back to his early days on the *Havannah*. How desperately he had planned to run away. Now was his chance, if he wanted it.

For a brief moment he seriously considered going. But why should he run away? Newport meant nothing to him any more. There was nobody there who cared about him. And it would mean letting down Mr Young and Emma. Suddenly, their friendship and respect meant more to him than anything in the world. He knew he would not let them down – he would endure Bosun Willett's bullying but he would not let his friends down.

At last Nat reached the market with its row upon row of brightly painted stalls. Sawdust covered the stone floor and pungent smells gripped his nostrils. Spices, fruit, cooked meats, rows of calico and cloth – a riot of colour and excitement surrounded him. He had to ask directions from one of the stall holders but soon he was standing in front of the stationer's shop.

A huge woman was serving. She glared at Nat but relaxed and smiled when he explained what he wanted.

'Mr Young told me to expect you,' she said, hands folded across her ample belly. 'Do you have the money?'

Nat passed across the sovereign and received in return two huge, leather bound volumes. The woman wrapped them carefully in brown paper and tied up the parcel with string.

'Don't drop them, now,' she said.

Nat shook his head and started off down the aisle.

'Here,' called the woman, suddenly.

Nat turned. She was smiling at him and holding out a big, red apple. He took it and bit into its shining surface. Waving his thanks he went happily down the aisle.

That was when he saw Bosun Willett. Nat stopped in his tracks, the apple halfway to his mouth, and in an instinctive movement ducked behind a stand of hanging cloth. He was not sure why he had done this – after all, he was here officially, the Bosun could not touch him. It was simply a reflex movement and the fear was suddenly huge in his belly.

When he peered out from his hiding place Nat was amazed to see that Bosun Willett was not alone. More importantly, he recognised the other man – it was Mr Best, the stranger who had first brought him to the *Havannah* all those months ago.

The two men were standing at the side of a large provisions stall and they were engaged in heated debate. Despite his fear Nat knew that he had to listen to what they were saying. Slowly, taking care to remain well hidden, he inched forward.

'We've got a deal, Bosun. And you're welching on it!'

Mr Best was obviously angry. His dark face was scowling and his heavy, black eyebrows were drawn together.

'I'm not welching on anything,' Willett retorted. 'We've got the bloody Home Office inspecting us tomorrow. I can't help it if I've got to give those brats the food they're supposed to have . . .'

'That's not my problem, Bosun. What am I supposed to sell here? Fresh air?'

Nat glanced at the stall behind Mr Best. Whatever he was selling, it certainly wasn't fresh air. Huge ham hocks, joints of beef and lamb, sacks of peas and other vegetables, overflowed from the stall. Dozens of eager shoppers crowded to buy their groceries.

Bosun Willett stared at Mr Best and slowly pointed his gnarled finger.

'Listen. If the Home Office decides the boys aren't being treated well, then they'll close the ship down. I'll lose my job and you'll get no more cheap provisions. And that way, you and I, we'll both miss out.'

He paused and stared at the crowd of shoppers clustering around the stall.

'We'll just have to put up with it for a week or so. 'Til after the inspection. 'Til Douglas Bloody Young loses interest again. A couple of weeks, that's all.'

Despite his anger, Mr Best could obviously see the sense in the Bosun's argument. He sighed and raised his arms in resignation. And at that moment his eyes fell on Nat. Eager to hear what was being said, the boy had pressed forward so that his face was now protruding between the rows of cloth. It would have been comical if the situation had not been so serious.

Mr Best frowned and motioned towards Nat.

'I say, isn't that one of your boys, Bosun?'

Nat took to his heels and ran. From behind him he heard a shout but he buried his head and kept running. He did not stop until he reached the River Taff. Panting, he looked back over his shoulder – there was no sign of pursuit.

He sat down on the river bank and thought about what he had seen. It was fairly obvious that Bosun Willett and Mr Best had set themselves up in business together. By keeping the *Havannah* boys on short rations they could supply themselves with cheap provisions and, from the size of the crowd around the stall, it seemed that there were plenty of people willing to buy the goods.

Nat had no idea what Mr Best did for a living. He presumed he was some official of the courts. Bosun Willett he knew all about, of course. Nat didn't suppose that running the stall as an extra form of income was illegal but, surely, stealing food from the *Havannah* was?

'So what do I do now?' he mused to himself.

Abstracted, he picked up a pebble and tossed it into the muddy water of the river. A huge ripple widened and spread across the surface.

Should he tell Mr Young? There was no evidence. At the moment the boys were being well fed and the Bosun would just deny everything. The past was the past. How could anybody prove what had happened the day or week before? Nobody would believe him or the other boys. They would just be regarded as troublemakers.

He thought, then, about running away. That would solve the problem for him. But it was also the cowardly way and for that reason he quickly discounted it. He would have to hold his information for the time being, he decided. The opportunity would surely come for him to use it. Timing; it was all about timing. He sprang to his feet and began walking down the river bank towards the dark bulk of the *Havannah*.

The Rev Sydney Turner arrived early the following day. He was a short man with a neatly-trimmed beard and he was accompanied by a fierce-looking woman who stared intently at everyone and everything.

'That's Mary Carpenter,' whispered Tommy Jenkins. 'I saw her picture in one of the magazines in the Games Room. She runs a Reformatory School in Bristol.'

Nat studied Miss Carpenter. She seemed to be an eager and dynamic woman but there was something else, something soft and caring, at the back of her eyes.

The two visitors were escorted all over the ship by Douglas Young and Bosun Willett. They sat and watched the boys in their nautical drills and at their lessons. Then Sydney Turner decided he would like to test some of the boys.

'One of your best, one of your worst, Mr Young,' Nat heard him say.

The Superintendent beckoned to Nat and he spent fifteen minutes reading and answering mental arithmetic questions for the Inspector.

'Well done, young man,' said Turner, at last. 'Most commendable.'

Nat was about to return to his seat when Mary Carpenter spoke.

'Wait. I would like to ask this boy a few questions.'

She raised her eyebrows at Mr Young. He nodded his approval.

'How long have you been here – Nat, is it?'

'Yes, Miss. Five months, Miss.'

Mary Carpenter nodded carefully.

'And how do you enjoy it here? Are you happy? You can speak freely.'

Nat glanced at Mr Young. He smiled back at the boy and spread his hands. He nodded approvingly.

'As Miss Carpenter says, you can speak freely, Nat.'

'I do enjoy it, Miss,' Nat said. 'I didn't at first, I didn't want to be here. But I like it now.'

'Is there anything you would like? Anything which is not being provided now?'

Nat shrugged.

'Some more food, Miss. We could always do with more to eat.'

He glanced across at Bosun Willett. Nat had not seen the Bosun since yesterday but now the man's face was red and glazed in a mixture of embarrassment and anger.

'These young boys,' he blustered quickly. 'Always, always after more.'

'Oliver Twist, Bosun?' said Mary Carpenter.

She stared at Willett. He was puzzled, not understanding this strange woman, and did not know how to reply. Miss Carpenter glared at him for several moments, then turned, smiling, to Nat.

'Thank you, Nat,' she said. 'That was most interesting.'

She knows, Nat thought, she knows what he's like. He went back to his seat and waited while Jimmy Baker was interrogated by Rev Turner. If Nat was the top of the school, Jimmy was the exact opposite. Yet Nat took no pleasure in seeing the boy stumble his way through the test. He hung his head until the Inspector had finished and glanced up only as Jimmy, red with shame, slouched back to his place.

'You wait, swot,' Jimmy hissed. 'You'll pay for this.'

Nat saw the Inspector and Miss Carpenter just once more before they left. That evening he made his way to Mr Young's cabin for his regular lesson and knocked lightly on the door. Emma threw it open almost immediately and quickly pulled him inside.

'The inspectors are just going. Father says to come in and wait.'

Nat nodded and stood quietly inside the door. Rev Turner and Miss Carpenter were making their farewells. As they crossed the room, Nat instinctively reached over and opened the door for them.

'Thank you, young man,' said Mary Carpenter. 'I take it you have come for your extra lessons?'

Nat was surprised that she knew but he quickly nodded his head.

'And do you really want to go to sea when you leave the *Havannah*?' asked Rev Turner.

Nat had not really thought about it properly, despite the pleasure he gained from the nautical training. He shrugged.

'I don't know, sir. I didn't when I first came – it was the last thing I wanted. But the training's been good. I enjoy it. And I love this ship. She's wonderful. So maybe I will go to the sea, maybe I will.'

'Seafaring is a good trade, boy,' said Mary Carpenter. 'Britain will always need sailors to supply the Empire. There are lots of openings in a port like Cardiff. Indeed, if any town in the country needs a nautical school, then it's this one. Take my advice, Nat. Go to sea.'

The two visitors swept out and Nat moved across the cabin to the wide stern window. He felt Emma by his side and glanced at her. The girl smiled at him and took his hand in hers. She squeezed gently and Nat returned the gesture.

The evening sun shone brightly on the hundreds of waiting ships out in the Bay, each of them with stories to tell, each of them with wonderful, exotic places to visit. Maybe he would go to sea, he thought. Maybe he would.

Chapter Six

JUNE 1870

Sunday was the only day of the week when the regular routine of the *Havannah* was relaxed. Bosun Willett would undoubtedly have preferred to keep the boys working but there were powers even greater than his and Home Office instructions simply had to be obeyed.

So on Sunday there was no school and no nautical training. The day was taken up with cleaning the ship and with religious services. Occasionally some of the boys would work, half-heartedly, on the vegetable patch which was being cultivated alongside the 'Havannah'. Mostly, however, the ship's company took the opportunity to relax and enjoy a little free time.

Nat usually spent Sunday afternoon in Douglas Young's cabin, reading one of the Superintendent's many books. True to his word, Mr Young had quickly got him reading the works of Charles Dickens and Nat, warming to the gentle encouragement and enthusiasm of his mentor, was soon devouring the books at a rapid rate. Often he and Emma would take turns at reading aloud while Douglas Young and the ever-present Miss Clarkson sat listening contentedly.

One day Mr Young reached up onto his book shelf and pulled out an old leather-bound volume. Carefully he passed it to Nat.

'Try that one,' Young said. 'Essential reading for any would-be sailor.'

Nat turned the book over in his hand and read the title page – *Robinson Crusoe* by Daniel Defoe. He shrugged and opened it to the first page.

From the first chapter Nat found himself drawn into a new and fabulous world. Crusoe's adventures and cruises, his long years marooned on the distant island, fascinated the boy and he read avidly. He knew now that he wanted to be a sailor. Books like *Robinson Crusoe* simply added to that desire.

And so he worked harder than ever at his nautical training. It did not please Bosun Willett. Nothing, it seemed, could help him with this martinet who simply sneered or snarled at him whenever they came into contact. Nat did not care. He had an ambition now, for the first time in his life, and nothing – or no one – would ever spoil that.

One Sunday towards the end of June, Nat was detailed for the morning church service on the upper deck. The day was beautifully fine and the time passed quickly. He came back to the dormitory to wash for dinner and found the place crowded with officers and boys. Everyone's possessions were strewn across the deck, long cherished photographs and momentos trampled and crushed underfoot.

'What's going on?'

'It's Bosun Willett,' hissed Tommy Jenkins, fear alive and burning in his eyes. 'He's lost his clasp knife. He says somebody's stolen it. They're searching all the lockers. We've got to stand by our bed space until they get round to us.'

A sense of foreboding, huge and tangible, engulfed Nat. His throat went dry and his tongue suddenly seemed too large for his mouth. He had never seen the Bosun's knife, but he knew, as surely as he knew his own name, that they would find it in his locker.

He stood alongside his rolled-up hammock and waited. Bosun Willett and several Officers were slowly making their way down the room, searching and throwing clothes everywhere. Once he caught the Bosun's eye and he could have sworn the man winked at him. Nat shook his head, as if to clear the vision, and when he looked again the Bosun was busy with somebody's locker. At last, however, it was his turn.

'You're next,' said Willett, his voice almost pleasant in the heavy atmosphere.

Nat shuddered with apprehension. Bosun Willett smiled, then suddenly sniffed in contempt. He reached down and threw open the lid of Nat's locker. It was exactly as the boy feared. There, on top of his small bundle of clothes, lay a huge, black-handled knife. The Bosun gleefully rubbed his hands together and carefully, almost delicately, reached for the weapon.

'Got you.'

He turned, grinning, towards Nat. The look of triumph and hate in his eyes would stay with the boy for as long as he lived. In that split second Nat realised he had been out-manoeuvred, that the Bosun had set him up. Now nobody would ever believe a word he said. Bosun Willett's secret was safe. A pang of regret flashed through his brain – why hadn't he told Mr Young when he had the chance?

'You thieving little ——!'

He heard the Bosun's voice and saw the man's huge fist begin to descend towards him. Before he could finish his words or his actions, Nat had reacted instinctively. He ducked underneath Willett's flailing arm and took to his heels. Boys and adults scattered before him as he sprinted away down the room.

'Stop that boy!' the Bosun screamed.

Nat had spent years dodging dockyard police and bands of rival street boys. Flat-footed instructors had no chance. Ducking and swerving like a snipe, he swept underneath the stowed hammocks, between piles of discarded clothes, away from the grasping hands.

He heard the familiar call of the hue and cry rising up like a trumpet wail behind him.

'Stop, thief!'

It was taken up by the Officers and then by the boys. Soon the whole ship rang with the shout.

'Stop thief! Stop thief!'

Within seconds Nat was out of the dormitory door and racing up the companionway to the main deck.

'We've got him cornered,' he heard Bosun Willett yell. 'There's no escape from up there. He's going nowhere.'

Too late, Nat realised that the man was right. The upper deck was mostly covered over and roofed in. Only at the very tip of the *Havannah*'s bow was there open space, where the deck opened out into the fresh air.

Nat heard feet pounding up the stairs behind him and knew he had to keep on running. He reached the upper deck and headed for the open bow. The *Havannah* normally sat, like a beached whale, on her mud bank but at high tide the bank was covered and sometimes the ship even floated free.

Now the dirty sludge of the River Taff slapped against the hull of the old vessel. Nat glanced, desperately, over the rail. It was almost an hour past high tide but how much water remained down there?

'Come here, you little bugger!'

He spun around. Bosun Willett and a mass of bodies clustered at the top of the companionway and along the deck. The nearest one was just ten feet away. Nat recognised Douglas Young close to the front of the group.

'You're for it now, boy!' Bosun Willett hissed.

Urgently, Nat searched for a way out. He saw the despair in Mr Young's face and, somehow, found the courage and the time to smile at him.

'Come on, Nat,' Young called. 'We can work this out.'

Nat turned and dived over the side of the ship. His stomach seemed to soar up, out of his body, and many months later, with hindsight, he would swear he had been falling for ten whole minutes. His body hit the river and he felt a terrible pain in the back of his head. Salt water and filthy mud choked his nose and mouth. Then he passed out.

The next thing Nat knew was the feel of cold mud, slimy and wet, against his face. It smelt awful, like rotten eggs. Tentatively, he sat up and twisted his neck around. His head hurt where he had smashed into the water but at least he could move. There seemed to be no serious damage.

He tried to stand but the mud was too deep and his arms sank up to the elbows in the slime. Staring out across the Bay he could see Penarth Head, a bare mile away, in the sunlight. The *Havannah* lay a few hundred yards up river, barely visible around a bend in the stream. He must have been carried here, to the edge of the Bay, Nat reasoned, by the tide.

There was no sign of pursuit from the ship. He sat and listened intently but there was only the usual morning sounds of voices on vessels, the metallic thump of clanging hammers and trains shunting. Even on Sundays the work did not stop.

'They must think I'm dead,' Nat muttered to himself. 'Maybe I should be, after a fall like that.'

A handful of seagulls and wading birds settled suddenly on the mud close by. The birds studiously ignored him, walking imperiously up and down the bank. Their cries were strident, echoing harshly across the Bay. It was time to move.

Carefully, Nat began to crawl across the mud towards the security of the nearby shore. It was hard going but, presently, he was able to pull himself up onto the shingle strand. He collapsed and lay panting, too tired to move further.

After a minute or so he began to gather his senses. Just because he could hear no sounds of pursuit, it did not mean that Officers from the *Havannah* were not, at that moment, out searching for him. They would surely be scouring the river bank for his body – Bosun Willett would delight in being absolutely sure that he was dead. He needed to move, quickly.

He pulled himself to his feet and began to trot off across the waste land which lay at the edge of the docks.

'Now where the Devil would you be going, my lad?'

Nat lurched to a sudden halt and looked quickly around. The voice was lilting and soft and came from close by. With a start he realised that there was a tramp sitting in the shade of an old thorn bush.

'Sorry?'

'I said, where the Devil would you be going on a fine morning like this?'

The man wore a long overcoat and his face was scarred by deep lines around the mouth. His hair was flaxen, almost yellow, and his eyes, Nat noticed, were soft and kind. After a moment he spoke again.

'I'm thinking that you're looking just a little bit wet. Wouldn't you agree?'

Nat shrugged.

'I, er, I fell in the water. I've got to go home and get dried off.'

'What, back there?'

The tramp gestured in the general direction of the *Havannah*.

'Oh, I recognise the uniform, lad. And I watched you come across the mud. Runaway, are you?'

Slowly Nat nodded. The tramp smiled and inclined his head. He held out a bottle.

'Come here and dry off in the sunshine, boy. Have a drink of water – it's only water, mind. Sorry I haven't got anything stronger.'

Nat hesitated, his eyes studying the tramp and gauging the distance to the edge of the clearing.

'Come on. I'm not going to turn you in. You're quite safe with me.'

Gingerly Nat took the outstretched bottle and drank deeply. He had not realised how thirsty he was. He gave the bottle back to the tramp and sat down beside him.

'I'm Fergus,' said the man, extending his hand. 'And who might you be?'

'Nat. Nat Thomas.'

'Captain Nat, is it? From HMS *Havannah*? Don't mind me, Captain, it's just my sense of humour. I'm from Ireland – as you can probably tell from my accent. God's own country, so it is. And God can keep it.'

He paused to take a deep swig from the bottle, then turned to face Nat again.

'Well, now, Captain Nat, a pretty little pickle, eh? I won't ask you why you've run away. We've all got reasons and secrets for everything we do. All of us. But just answer me this – are you going back?'

Nat shook his head. He couldn't ever go back, not now. And at that moment a black wave of despair came down across his life. The Bosun had set him up – probably using Jimmy Baker to plant the knife. Now everybody thought he had stolen it and he would never get a fair hearing. Even Mr Young would think him guilty. And Emma. At the thought of it his eyes began to moisten and he hastily wiped away a tear.

'No,' he said. 'I'm never going back.'

The tramp nodded, wistfully.

'Fine. Then let's go and get some dinner.'

Still Nat was dubious. He hesitated and Fergus grinned. He shrugged his shoulders.

'Sure, you don't need to come. I understand. But don't worry, I don't mean you no harm. I'm hungry and I'm damned sure you are, too.'

He climbed easily to his feet.

'Look, Nat – Captain Nat – I'm a great believer in fate. Fate sent you here, I think. You could be useful to me. You and me, I think we might just make a good team – seeing as you're not going back to that there ship of yours. You've got to eat to stay alive, haven't you.'

'I suppose so,' Nat said.

'Well then, how about this partnership? People always give better – give more, so to speak – if there's a kid in the case. Me and my gift of the gab, you with those angelic looks of yours. You help me, I help you. That's the way of it, as I see it. Nothing permanent, like, just as long as it suits us both.'

Nat knew the man was right. He was on the streets again, now, and he needed to survive as best he could. He would need friends like Fergus. So he nodded and stood up alongside the man.

The rest of the day passed in something of a haze. He sat with Fergus, eating oranges they had filched from some sacks at the side of a dock. He dried himself in front of an enormous fire which a band of vagrants had lit on wasteland just outside the dock gates. Fergus seemed to know them and Nat, as the Irishman's companion, was accepted without question.

For hours Nat sat there, gazing into the flames, wondering how he could have been so stupid. He should have reported Bosun Willett days or weeks ago, then none of this need have happened.

He knew he should get away, well away from the docks, from Cardiff and anybody who might recognise him. And yet he couldn't. He had nowhere to go and, more important, there was something holding him, some invisible force or power which kept him close to the river and to the *Havannah*.

'Here, boy,' growled Fergus later that evening. 'Put this on.'

He threw a dirty, old blanket at Nat and the boy gratefully draped it around his shoulders. It stank and was full of holes but the fire had begun to die and he knew that, sleeping in the open air for the first time in many months, he would soon need it.

Nat lay and tried to sleep. The ground was hard beneath his back and he missed the easy swing of his hammock. Despite the discomfort of the Industrial School, he didn't want to be anywhere else. The *Havannah* had been his one chance to climb out of the trap of poverty and crime. Now he had lost it forever.

The only thing he could do was to stay close to the ship. And that, at least, gave him pleasure. Her safety and security might be gone but at least by being close he could remember what it had been like. Remember and regret with every ounce of his soul.

Chapter Seven

JUNE TO AUGUST 1870

For the next few weeks Nat hung aimlessly around the streets of Cardiff and the docks. The group of vagrants seemed to have made themselves a temporary home outside the dock gates. Nobody bothered them, the police and dock officials preferring to live in mutual harmony with their unexpected visitors rather than wage open warfare. A fire usually blazed in the centre of the camp and Nat knew that he was always welcome around its warming glow.

Together with Fergus he trudged the streets, begging for money or doing odd jobs like carrying bags outside the stations and hotels. It was hard going, despite the Irishman's patter. Sometimes Nat stole oranges and apples from the market barrows or stalls. For years he had stolen to keep himself alive and had never given the rights or wrongs of it a second thought. It had simply been something he had to do.

Now, however, it felt wrong. He knew there was another way – the *Havannah* had taught him that much.

'Steal or starve, boy,' Fergus would shrug. 'It's your choice.'

And so Nat had filched the fruit and run. He knew it was a backward step but he had no choice.

On some days he would squat for hours on the river bank and watch the *Havannah* boys as they rowed their longboat up and down the Taff. He was often able to pick out Tommy Jenkins and the others. His ginger haired friend was unmistakable with his shock of red hair standing out vertically from his head – like a parrot's comb, Nat decided.

He did not wave or shout. To do so would have spelt disaster. So he kept his peace and a huge wave of sorrow would invariably rise up in his heart.

Once he saw Bosun Willett kicking and punching unmercifully at someone who had missed his stroke.

'You stupid, useless boy!' the Bosun roared, his voice carrying across the mud of the Bay. 'God knows why I bother trying to teach you anything.'

The old hatred rose again in Nat but he was powerless to help or intervene. He had no purpose in life any more. The *Havannah* had been his only chance to succeed and it hurt to see his friends treated so badly.

Early one morning, several weeks later, Nat was slouching back to the vagrants' camp after a fruitless hunt for breakfast. He hoped Fergus had been more successful – otherwise it promised to be another hungry day.

He trudged down Bute Street and, with his hands thrust into his pockets, turned the corner towards the docks. At that moment he came face to face with Bosun Willett and Mr Best. The shock was like a blow to the solar plexus.

The two men were in deep conversation and, for a few seconds, Nat remained unnoticed. He began to inch back towards the corner but the movement was enough to attract Mr Best's attention. He looked up and started. Slowly he pointed his arm at Nat.

'Bosun? It's that boy again.'

Willett's head jerked around. Astonishment was written across his face – he really had believed that the boy was dead.

'Nat Thomas,' he breathed. 'By all that's Holy. Alive and kicking, after all!'

He lunged forward, huge hands grasping for Nat's jumper. The boy jumped backwards and, for a moment, the Bosun was caught off balance. Nat turned, ready to run, but cannoned into the pillar of the building behind him and fell heavily onto the pavement.

He felt, rather than saw, Bosun Willett loom above him and rolled desperately sideways as the expected boot flew towards him. The Bosun's kick took Nat on the side of his thigh. He winced at the pain and then his grasping hands caught hold of a long piece of wood, the splintered remains of a packing case which was lying against the building. Instantly he was on his feet, swinging the makeshift club in front of him.

'Keep away!' he screamed.

Bosun Willett and Mr Best fell back a few feet, both of them staring at the weapon. Desperately Nat glanced around. Three or four hundred yards away, with their backs towards him, a group of drunken sailors were returning to their ship after a night on the town. Apart from them the street was deserted. The Bosun followed Nat's gaze and smiled grimly.

'That's right, boy, there's nobody to help you. You're on your own. And this time I'm not going to stop at six strokes of a bloody birch cane.'

Nat saw murder in his eyes and was suddenly afraid. He knew, instinctively, that the man had nothing to lose. Everybody on the *Havannah* believed him dead already.

To take him back to the ship would mean questions – much better to finish him off and dump his body in the dock.

He stared at the Bosun. Willett grinned again, as if he could sense Nat's thoughts and slowly nodded his head.

'That's right, boy,' he breathed. 'This is the end of the road.'

At that moment a whirling dervish swept around the corner. It flashed past Nat and cannoned into Mr Best and the Bosun, sending the two men crashing to the ground. Nat watched, fascinated, as Mr Best's black top hat rolled away into the centre of the road.

'Run, boy!' screamed Fergus, taking to his heels and disappearing down the long street.

Quickly gathering his senses, Nat raced off after his rescuer. He did not look back until he had gone half a mile. Then Fergus pulled up, panting and dragging on his arm.

'Hold it, Nat. For God's sake, boy, I'm not as fit as I was. They're not chasing us – you're safe.'

They stood, leaning against an empty shop front, gasping for breath. Fergus, bent over and blowing, sounded like a set of bagpipes. Slowly, however, he straightened up and began to grin. Playfully, he nudged Nat in the ribs.

'Sure but that was good fun, wasn't it? I think now, maybe, it's about time you told me what this is all about.'

Nat nodded. Fergus was right. He had just saved Nat's life, so he deserved to be told. Slowly, they walked on and, as they went, Nat told him the story. He told it all, everything from his arrival on board the *Havannah* to the extra lessons with Mr Young and

71

Bosun Willett's growing hatred. The vagrant was mostly silent, listening intently and giving Nat his full attention. Occasionally he asked a question or clarified a point but mainly he kept his peace.

Eventually, Nat came to the story of the dark-suited man. He told Fergus about the market stall and the stolen provisions and about how he had been set up as a thief.

'So nobody knows about the Bosun and this Mr Best? Nobody apart from you, that is?'

Nat nodded.

'Then you're in a tricky position, lad. As I see it – and this is just my opinion, mind you – his only security lies in you being out of the way. When he thought you were dead then he was happy enough. But now that he knows you're not, he's going to be even more frightened. And even more dangerous.'

'So what should I do?'

Fergus shrugged. He pursed his lips and did not speak for a few minutes.

'About the Bosun? There's not a whole lot you can do,' he said eventually. 'Nothing that's going to get him off your back, that's for sure. I think the only choice you've got is to actually tell somebody.'

He paused and carefully nodded his head.

'Yes, tell somebody. I think that's the answer. Somebody who'll believe you. Not me, mind you. I don't count. I'm just a nobody, an Irish tinker. You need to tell somebody who has a bit of clout. They might not be able to help you just now – or maybe not ever – but at least by them knowing it's a degree of safety. That way, if anything did happen to you, anything fatal, so to speak . . .'

He left the sentence unfinished but caught Nat's eye and shrugged.

'But what's the point of telling anybody?' Nat queried. 'Surely it's too late for that?'

'Not at all,' said Fergus. 'It may not help you – I mean, you'd be dead, wouldn't you? But if you did tell somebody, tell it all, including your fears – you know, him wanting you dead and all that – at least that way if you did die it would be some consolation, wouldn't it?'

Nat frowned; the Irishman's logic was beyond him.

'Listen,' Fergus continued. 'They'd put two and two together, the Authorities, the law, that is. They'd know you were telling the truth, after all.'

Reluctantly, Nat decided that Fergus was right. It was the only option open to him. But who could he tell? Mr Young? No, he would have to believe the Bosun, all the evidence was in his favour. And besides, Mr Young always seemed to let Willett do whatever he liked. He wasn't strong enough, not by a long shot.

'What about that little friend of yours,' said Fergus. 'The Superintendent's daughter. Emma? You said she understood about the Bosun.'

Nat frowned. On the face of it Emma seemed the logical choice. She was his friend and she knew what Bosun Willett was like. Yet should he place her in such a dangerous position? And it *would* be dangerous if Bosun Willett knew that she knew. Unfortunately, he could think of nobody else. Fergus nodded.

'She doesn't need to say anything to anybody. Certainly not the Bosun. It's just protection, in case anything does happen to you. But then again, maybe she can drop in the odd word here and there. To her father, like, or anybody else who can help. You never know.'

He would do it, Nat decided. Perhaps Emma would be able to put in a good word for him with her father. That was if she didn't hate him – if she didn't believe him to be a thief. He shook his head, not wanting to believe that Emma could think badly of him. He *would* tell her, but the time had to be right.

Now that he had decided, Nat suddenly realised he desperately wanted to see Emma again, to let her know that he was still alive. She would believe him, she was bound to. He could hardly wait.

He began to watch the *Havannah* carefully, taking pains to stay well out of sight of anybody on board. Day after day he haunted the river banks around the ship. He knew it was dangerous but there seemed to be no other way.

Two or three times he managed to catch a glimpse of Emma but she was always with Miss Clarkson or her father. It seemed that he would never be able to get her alone.

Finally, one hot August Sunday afternoon when the sun baked the tar on the roads and on the side of the ship, causing it to bubble and pop like pools of sulphur, Nat got his chance. He was sitting behind an old tin shed at the top of the path which led down to the *Havannah*, when he heard somebody coming across the cinders. Squinting out from his hiding place, he was amazed to see that it was Emma. She was dressed in a white frock and carried a huge parasol to keep off the sun. More importantly, she was alone.

'Emma?' he called.

The girl spun around, shock and amazement written across her face. Then she laughed, delightedly, and ran towards him.

'Nat. Oh, Nat. I knew you weren't dead. I just knew it.'

She hugged him tightly but Nat pulled away and held her at arms length.

'No,' he said. 'You'll dirty your dress. I'm filthy. Just look at me.'

She shook her head and hugged him again.

'I don't care. It's just so good to see you. Are you all right? Where have you been? Oh, Nat, there's so much I want to ask you.'

He took her hand and led her away from the *Havannah*. Finding a secluded spot beside a warehouse, Nat sat down and inclined his head for Emma to do the same.

'How long have you got? I need to talk to you but it'll take half an hour, at least.'

'It's all right,' Emma smiled. 'I'm supposed to be on my way to Sunday School. Miss Clarkson is ill so I've been allowed to go on my own. We've got an hour, maybe more.'

Nat nodded and began his tale. Emma listened, intently and seriously, with all the wisdom of an older woman. Only once did she interrupt his flow.

'I knew it,' she exclaimed when he told her about the knife incident. 'I knew you wouldn't have stolen a silly old knife. I told my father but he kept saying "Evidence, Emma, evidence." I knew you hadn't stolen it. And I knew you were alive, I just knew it.'

Nat smiled at her and held up his hand to stop her.

'All right,' she grinned. 'All right. Carry on.'

He told her about Fergus and his friends among the tramps, and finally he told her about Bosun Willett. Bright circles of colour rose to Emma's cheeks.

'That awful man. He really is the limit – I could just kill him, I really could.'

Nat stared at her. Anger and contempt pooled in her eyes and he knew that he had been right to seek her out.

'Fergus was right, you had to tell someone. I'm glad you chose me, Nat, really glad. But we've got to be careful. I don't know how we can catch Bosun Willett but we will. Somehow. We'll just have to wait for our chance.'

'Never mind catching the Bosun,' Nat protested. 'He's too clever to get caught. I'm only telling you all this in case anything should happen to me. Then at least you know the truth – perhaps you can do something with it. You or your father.'

Emma was suddenly afraid and it showed in her face.

'Don't talk like that. Nothing is going to happen to you, Nat, nothing at all.'

If only I could be sure, Nat thought, but with Bosun Willett you never knew. Emma took his hand and squeezed it gently.

'We will catch him out, Nat. Sooner or later he'll make a slip. We'll be ready when he does.'

The hour passed all too quickly, and, at last, the time came for Emma to return to the *Havannah*. Nat walked with her to the top of the cinder path.

'I can't come any further,' he said. 'You never know who might be watching.'

Emma smiled, wistfully.

'We'll find a way out of this, Nat, really we will. It's going to be all right. I know where to find you now, if I need you.'

She leaned forward and kissed him lightly on the top of his head. Nat felt the colour rise to his cheeks but he knew that he was glad she had done it. He stood and watched her skip down the path, then turned away and went back to the vagrant camp.

For the first time in months he felt happy.

Chapter Eight

AUGUST 1870

The attack began at about 3.00 am, the empty nothing of the night. Nat had just drifted off to sleep, lulled by the dying flames of the camp fire into a world of harsh dreams and soft images. Visions of his mother and Emma, the *Havannah* and Bosun Willett, were mixed and jumbled around his unconscious brain. He mumbled and moaned and was unaware that Fergus gently laid his hand upon his head and kept it there until the moment had passed.

He was jolted awake by a piercing scream. The next second a shower of rocks and boulders crashed down onto the sleeping vagrants and the area around the fire was filled with running shapes. Cries and shrieks echoed around the clearing as Nat sat up, blanket draped around his shoulders, wondering what on earth was going on.

'Look for the boy!' he heard somebody shout. 'It's the boy we want. Look for the boy.'

Dimly, as if from far away, came the realisation that the urgent words were about him. He shook his head and threw off the blanket. All around him men were fighting, clubbing each other with sticks and fists, their screams and shouts filling the night air. Suddenly, Fergus was by his side.

'Come away, Nat,' he hissed. 'Time we weren't here.'

Together, they eased out of the firelight. Suddenly, a huge shape loomed up in front of them and, strangely, he heard Fergus sigh. It was a low, quiet sound, filled with resignation and despair.

'Where the Devil do you think you're going, Irish? Walk away, now, and you'll not be hurt. Just leave the boy where he is.'

Fergus was staring intently at the shape in front of him, the man who had just spoken. He breathed in and spread his arms out wide, the very picture of ease and affability.

'Now, Jemmy,' he said, pleasantly, 'why would I be doing that?'

The other man lurched forward and Fergus quickly pushed Nat behind him. He did not give ground and Nat was suddenly aware of a hardening in his attitude.

'It's the boy we want, Irish,' said the man. 'Not you. We've got no fight with you. Just give us the boy and we'll be on our way.'

Fergus shrugged and Nat knew, without seeing his face, that he was smiling that dangerous smile of his. Yet the big man, this Jemmy as Fergus had called him, saw only the smile, not the danger.

'Now you know I can't do that, Jemmy,' said Fergus. 'The boy stays with me. If you want him you'll have to try and take him.'

Jemmy hesitated, uncertain. That was his big mistake. As swift as lightning Fergus leapt forward and his fists flashed. Once, twice, he hit the big man – smack on the point of his chin – and that was enough. Jemmy collapsed in the dirt. Fergus stared, briefly, at his fallen shape and turned towards Nat. Apologetically, he shrugged.

'I don't like doing that. But, sure, they never learn.'

He took Nat by the arm and gently pulled him away from the conflict. The darkness was both a shield and a cover and nobody noticed their going. When they came to a nearby stack of timber, Fergus pushed Nat down behind it, searched around for a weapon and came up with a large club of wood.

'Now, you stay here, Captain Nat,' he grinned. 'Me, I'm going to enjoy myself for a few minutes.'

He bounded away. Nat watched his tall shape dance into the yellow glow of the firelight where men were still hunting and fighting. Three times he saw Fergus strike with the club and each time another body lay stretched out, motionless, on the earth.

Suddenly, however, came the distant sound of police whistles.

'It's the law,' he heard someone shout. 'The law's coming.'

Nat saw the battered shape of Jemmy, Fergus's earlier opponent, stagger into the firelight. He looked as if he was drunk, Nat decided.

'Come on, lads,' Jemmy called. 'Leave it there.'

In a matter of seconds the camp emptied of figures – tramps and their assailants alike. One moment the scene was filled with fighting, flailing bodies; the next it was empty of all human life. Even the wounded or unconscious men were spirited away by their comrades.

Fergus's voice, when it came, was sharp and urgent and it made him jump. It came from close behind him.

'Keep still, Nat. Don't say a word.'

He felt Fergus's hand on his shoulder and knew that he would be safe as long as this strange, laughing Irishman was there beside him. Together they watched as half a dozen dockyard policemen edged warily into the camp and began to root amongst the packing cases and blankets. It was a fruitless exercise and after ten minutes they happily gave up and wandered back to their base. Slowly, the vagrants began to drift back towards the camp fire.

'We'll sleep here tonight, Nat,' Fergus instructed. 'I'll go and get your blanket. Got to keep you warm – you're obviously a very important person, so you are.'

Nat watched him wander over to the fire. Soon he was engaged in deep conversation with another of the vagrants. Nat's eyes began to close and when the Irishman came back, ten minutes later, he was already fast asleep.

The following morning there was bread and coffee for breakfast. Nat was amazed.

'Sure if one of them fellows last night didn't have a couple of sovereigns in his pocket,' laughed Fergus. 'I just – er – lightened him a little!'

Nat grinned and helped himself to coffee from the tin suspended over the fire. Several of the vagrants were sporting bruises this morning, he noticed, and one of them had his arm in a makeshift sling. The police had obviously decided to stay well clear of the camp.

He drank his coffee while Fergus and several of the tramps conferred with each other. The discussion, he noticed, was long and intense.

After a while Nat dozed in front of the eternal fire. His half dreams were peopled with thugs and fist fights, with Bosun Willett and the dark-suited Mr Best. Always, at the edge of his imaginings, however, there was Emma, smiling warmly in his direction.

He woke suddenly to feel Fergus's hand on his shoulder.

'Little bit of information for you, Captain Nat. From what we can gather that wee pantomime last night was paid for and set up by your friend Bosun Willett. We managed to sweat that out of one of their wounded men.'

It came as no great surprise. After all, they had said who they were after. Who else but Bosun Willett would organise such a raid?

'He must be pretty desperate,' said Fergus. 'And more to the point, he'll probably try again.'

'You really think so?'

'Oh yes. Most of those thugs last night came from the pubs and taverns of Tiger Bay. For the price of a few pints he can gather himself an army any time he wishes.'

Nat considered Fergus's words. The man was probably right. He was about to say so when Fergus spoke again.

'So we've decided to scarper. Now, before it all gets too hot for us. We don't need too many episodes like last night. We want to live in peace with the law – a few more set-to's like that and the peelers will be breathing down our necks every minute of the day.'

Nat was stunned. Was Fergus really talking about leaving? He didn't understand.

'You can't run away,' he managed to gasp, at last. 'You can't. You gave them a good beating last night, you can do it again.'

'Sure we can,' said Fergus. 'But like I said, that's trouble we really don't need. Oh look, Nat, we were going soon anyway. The hop-picking starts in Kent in a few weeks and we can make enough there to see us through the winter. We just don't *need* to stay here.'

Nat was on his feet now, a real panic beginning to claw at his belly. If Fergus left he would be at the mercy of Bosun Willett. Anything could happen. Fergus, however, was already ahead of him.

'Come with us, Nat. We're a good team, you and I. You've got no reason to stay here – plenty of good reasons for going, though. Come with us. The lads are happy enough about it. You're one of them, as far as they're concerned.'

It was the way out, the obvious road to take. With Fergus and his friends he had a place, they accepted him for what he was – even liked him for it. What earthly reason was there for him to stay here? Branded a thief, sentenced to an Industrial School and faced by the very real threat of physical harm or even death – why the Devil should he stay?

'I . . . I . . . don't know,' he stammered. 'Wales is my home. I belong here.'

'Really?' said Fergus, his eyes widening. 'Nobody belongs in a place like this. To a life of crime. Do they?'

He shrugged and turned away. Then he stopped and glanced back over his shoulder.

'Think about it, Nat. We'll be going first thing tomorrow morning. You think about it and let me know.'

Nat spent the day on the river bank, turning the matter over and over in his head. The two choices were obvious – to go or to stay.

To stay meant further persecution from Bosun Willett, maybe even death. It was undoubtedly the dangerous choice. Willett would never give up – last night's attack had proved that, beyond any shadow of a doubt. He was a worried, frightened man and, as Fergus had said, that made him doubly dangerous.

To go meant safety, at least for the time being. Bosun Willett's influence was strictly local, he would not follow him to Kent. Yet it also meant that his name would never be cleared. All his friends – Mr Young, Tommy, old Miss Clarkson – would always believe he was a thief. To go was easy but it was also the coward's way.

And so he made his decision. He would stay.

That evening he walked back to the camp and sought out his friend. Fergus was philosophical about his news.

'Fair enough, young man. I'll miss you but you've got to do what you think is right. What I want is neither here nor there. Just promise me one thing – you'll look after yourself?'

Nat nodded. 'I'll try,' he said.

They set a guard that night as they settled down, for the last time, in front of the camp fire. As Fergus said, Bosun Willett probably wouldn't try again, quite so soon, but it was best to take no chances.

Nat slept very little. Memories and fears flashed in and out of his brain. So much seemed to have happened in the past few months, it was hard to keep his jumbled thoughts from running total riot. Now the one person he had counted on to protect him – the only person, apart from Emma, who seemed to care – was about to leave. Nat was suddenly afraid, afraid of the future and all it might bring.

Several times during the night he woke with a start, panic clawing at his stomach and heart. Each time he woke he saw Fergus sitting straight and alert, wide awake beside the fire.

'Don't worry, Nat,' the Irishman said once, the last time he woke, just before dawn. 'They'll not come now.'

They didn't. The morning was dry and bright and from the crack of dawn the camp was a hive of activity as the vagrants began to pack together their few possessions. Fergus brewed up the last of the coffee and passed it across.

'Finish this off, Nat. You'll need it. We've got lots of places to call, favours to collect, on the march. You finish that off.'

He smiled and raised his eyebrows.

'Not changed your mind, by any chance?'

Nat shook his head but did not trust himself to speak.

'I didn't think you would,' said Fergus.

All too soon it was time for the group to leave. Nat stood alongside the fire as they trudged past, calling out to him and raising their arms in farewell. Fergus was the last to go.

'May the road always rise to meet you, Nat,' he said and pulled the boy close to hug him.

Then he was gone, away from the fire and the dock gates, towards whatever the future might hold. For a minute or two Nat could hear his loud, tuneless whistle beyond the curve of the dock wall. Slowly it faded and his last contact with the Irishman was over.

Nat sat in front of the fire, filled with an incredible sadness. He was alone now and more lonely than he had ever been in his whole existence. The last warmth and comfort, the last human contact, seemed to have gone from his life. The docks and the muddy water of Cardiff Bay seemed colder and less friendly that they had ever been.

Chapter Nine

SEPTEMBER 1870

The next few weeks were not easy for Nat. He scavenged and stole enough food to survive and, as far as possible, tried to live out of sight. He needed to stay hidden, he reasoned. That way Bosun Willett might think he had gone with the rest of the vagrants and stop looking for him – at least for a little while.

He missed Fergus, missed hearing his broad Irish brogue and bellowing laugh. He missed his friendship and protection and hoped, desperately, that some day he might get to see the man again. Often he was close to despair, his longing for care and compassion almost overwhelming him.

'Have you gone forever, Fergus?' he called aloud, one day.

His voice echoed out across the waters of Cardiff Bay. Only the scream of wheeling seagulls answered him and he knew, now, that he was truly alone.

Once Emma came to the old camp site outside the dock gates. He watched her from a distance but did not shout or make himself known. Better for her not to know where he was, he thought, she was already too deeply involved in this dangerous business.

When the sorrow and loneliness began to overwhelm him, Nat knew that there was only one place to find solace. He could not explain it but the *Havannah* seemed to be the single piece of constancy in his life. As September slowly died he found himself being drawn more and more often to the vicinity of the old ship.

He knew it was dangerous, knew that if anybody recognised him he would be instantly seized and thrashed. If Bosun Willett ever happened to meet him or see him in the distance then the hunt would begin again. And this time there was no Fergus, no band of beggars to help him out. Yet he could not help himself, he had to be close to the old ship.

Usually, if the night was dry, he would squat on the grassy margins of the river bank below the vessel, wrapped in his dirty old blanket. He would stay there until dawn began to break and people started to move about above his head. Then he would slip away and try to find food for the day.

One Saturday morning he was crouched, as usual, shivering inside his blanket. The light was dismal and grey but at least it had been a dry night. He stretched and tried to rub some feeling back into his cold limbs.

'I expect they're warm on the *Havannah*,' he breathed. 'Warm and safe.'

At that moment he heard a voice from the ship above. He started with fear, thinking that he had misjudged the time and that somebody had seen him. But no, the city, away to his right, was silent and still as death. No ships moored or hooted their sirens in the docks and the *Havannah* lay like a beached whale above him. It was so quiet that when the voice spoke again he heard the words quite plainly, even though they were hushed in silent and urgent whisper.

'Here,' somebody said. 'Put that tar here.'

Instantly, Nat froze. Tar? What did they want tar for? And what was anybody on the *Havannah* doing up and about at this time of day? Even Bosun Willett rarely woke before five-thirty. The voice had come from low down on the ship's hull, from a point almost directly above Nat's head. He craned his ears and then, low and menacing, the voice came again.

'Who's got the kindling?'

Nat leapt to his feet in a frenzy. Tar and kindling, at this time of the morning? Somebody was trying to set fire to the ship.

All thoughts of safety went out of his mind immediately. Only one thing mattered – to save the *Havannah*. Almost before he knew what he was doing Nat took to his heels, racing along the towpath, up and over the wooden gangway which led into the landlocked vessel. The door was firmly bolted but he kicked at it in a frenzy and screamed at the top of his voice.

'Let me in! Open up!'

Within a few seconds a bleary-eyed watchman threw open the door and stood before him.

'What do you want?' he demanded, scratching his head and blinking in the early light. 'Causing mayhem at this time of day. Go away!'

Nat ignored him and shouldered his way into the entry port. The watchmen fell back against the door frame.

'Hey!' he called. 'You can't come in here like that. Stop there!'

Moving quickly, Nat raced along the companionways, the night watchman panting behind him. Douglas Young lived at the stern of the ship, alongside his office and close to the point where the hidden fire raisers were, even now, at work. It seemed like hours but, at last, he arrived, gasping from his exertions, at the cabin. He hammered on the door.

'Mr Young. Sir. Quickly, come quickly!'

He heard the night watchman coming hurriedly down the passageway behind him and, for a moment, thought that the game was up. Then the door swung open and Douglas Young stood there, yawning, still tying the cord of his purple dressing gown.

'Nat,' he gasped, suddenly wide awake. 'Nat Thomas. Where the Devil have you sprung from?'

Behind the Superintendent, Nat saw Emma emerge from her bedroom, woken by the noise and shouting. Her hair was dishevelled and she was still half asleep but he found time to smile at her before turning again to Mr Young.

'Quick, sir,' he urged. 'Fire. There's a fire.'

'What on earth are you talking about, Nat?' asked Mr Young. 'There's no fire here.'

'Listen to him, father,' said Emma, laying her hand on Young's arm. 'If Nat says there's a fire, you'd better believe him.'

Nat turned, evaded the watchman's grasping arms and danced away down the companionway.

'Come on, sir!' he called.

Douglas Young and the night watchman chased after him. Down into the bowels of the ship they went, deeper and deeper into the murky hull. On the lowest deck Mr Young suddenly paused and sniffed the air.

'Smoke,' he declared.

He reached forward and threw open a nearby bulkhead door. At the far end of the compartment three boys were crouched over a mound of wood, old clothes and tar. They had built up their fire against the bulkhead wall and a glowing mass of flame was, at that very moment, beginning to blaze and billow.

'Stop!' called Mr Young.

At the sound of the Superintendent's voice the boys swung around and Nat recognised the swarthy features of Jimmy Baker. Panic flashed across his face as he and his two friends fell back a pace or two. Their shock was short-lived, however.

'Run!' screamed Jimmy.

He put down his head and powered for the doorway. The night watchman tried to grab him but Jimmy's head caught him in the midriff and the man fell away, gasping.

Strangely detached, Nat realised that Jimmy was heading directly for him. All the anger, pain and sorrow of the past few months suddenly welled up inside Nat. He knew what he had to do.

He gathered himself and when Jimmy was barely two feet away swung his fist with every last ounce of strength he possessed. The blow caught Jimmy on the point of his jaw. The big boy somersaulted backwards and lay, prostrate, on the deck.

Nat shook his fist. It had hurt but it had been well worth it.

'Fergus would have been proud of that one,' he breathed to himself.

The other two boys stood back against the bulkhead, their eyes fixed on Jimmy's fallen body. They had no intention of suffering a similar fate.

'Jonas,' called Mr Young to the watchman. 'Put out that fire.'

He turned and beckoned to the two boys.

'You two – pick him up and follow me.'

There was a sudden harshness in his voice that Nat had never heard before. As the night watchman, still groaning and holding his stomach, moved to extinguish the fire, the two boys walked obediently towards Jimmy and pulled him to his feet.

The next few hours passed quickly. Nat was escorted to Mr Young's cabin and left there, with the door firmly bolted. He sat on the wooden bench beneath the wide stern window and stared out at the ships in Cardiff Bay. The day's work had now begun and the ships were full of running men. Huge sailing vessels eased in and out of the docks, their decks filled to overflowing with cargo and passengers. It was like any normal day and yet, to Nat and the *Havannah*, it was anything but normal.

After an hour the Superintendent came to question him. He was accompanied by a police inspector and Emma. Eagerly the girl sat down beside him on the bench.

'It's time you told Daddy everything, Nat. I've told him what I know but he still needs to hear it from you.'

She gazed at him, smiling. Slowly Nat nodded and started his tale. Young and the policeman listened and, when he had finished, began to question him. Again and again the questions flew.

'So where do you say this market stall is located?' asked the inspector, eventually. 'This place that Mr Best and the Bosun run?'

'Right next to the stationer's, sir. Where Mr Young sent me. That's where I saw them – where they saw me.'

The police inspector left the room and for another forty minutes Nat was left alone. Emma squeezed his arm as she went out with her father and winked at him from the doorway.

When the door flew open next, Mr Young's face was wreathed in smiles.

'The inspector has been to the market, Nat. And who should he see there but Mr Best. Just like you said.'

'He's confessed everything,' Emma laughed, delightedly, dancing around Nat. 'Everything. He and the Bosun were in partnership, just as you said. They were making a fortune for themselves.'

Douglas Young nodded and sat behind his desk. The police inspector took one of the chairs.

'Unfortunately, what Emma says is true,' Young said. 'They were selling food and clothes which should have been yours, yours and the other boys on board the *Havannah*. I'm afraid I've been rather blind.'

'Ahem?'

The inspector coughed, quietly, bringing Young's head sharply around.

'The Bosun? Perhaps we'd better have him in now?'

Mr Young nodded and motioned Nat to a chair at the far side of the room. He and Emma sat obediently.

'Stay there, Nat and, whatever happens, don't say a word.'

Young rang a bell on his desk and a few moments later Bosun Willett ghosted in through the door. Somebody had obviously told him there was danger afoot. His face was white with apprehension and he looked, Nat thought, like an old man. For the very first time he seemed almost vulnerable.

'You've heard about the attempted arson, Bosun?'

said Douglas Young. 'Jimmy Baker and a few of his cronies. They're locked in the brig for the moment. We've questioned them once but the inspector, here, will want fuller statements in a short while.'

'Of course,' said Willett. 'Terrible. Terrible. I don't know what the boy was thinking about.'

Young nodded. He toyed, idly, with a paper weight on his desk, then suddenly looked up into the Bosun's eyes.

'That's not the reason we wanted to see you. What we'd really like to know about is your relationship with Mr Best.'

From his seat in the corner of the cabin, Nat saw a sudden spasm of anguish shoot across the Bosun's face. The man's mouth opened and closed, as if he was gasping for air, but nothing came out. He swallowed two or three times and finally, after a supreme effort, managed to blurt out a few words.

'Mr Best? From the court? Nothing – I don't have a relationship with him.'

The police inspector stood up and walked around the desk.

'We know it all, Bosun. Nat has told us everything.'

As he spoke he gestured with his hand and Bosun Willett glanced towards Nat. He had not seen the boy before, had not been aware of his presence. Now, for the first time he realised the enormity of the situation. His eyes met Nat's and once again the old hatred blazed out.

'Him?' he stormed. 'You don't believe a brat like him? A vagrant and a thief?'

He lurched forward but the inspector blocked his path. There was a brief struggle and then the Bosun dropped, exhausted, into a chair. He knew that he could not get to Nat and the knowledge destroyed him.

'You can't believe him,' he mumbled. 'You can't.'

'Oh, but we do, Mr Willett.'

The Bosun stared up at the inspector, his face working and chest heaving. The policeman leaned close and spoke softly but urgently into his ear.

'More to the point, your partner – Mr Best? – has already confessed everything. But I think, now, that I need to talk to you about something far more serious than petty theft.'

He straightened up and walked to the back of the Bosun's chair. Willett stared around the room, his eyes unable to focus.

'I need to talk to you,' said the inspector, 'about violent attacks on this boy. Life-threatening attacks. And I think we had best do that at the police station, don't you?'

There was a sharp click and before he had time to move the Bosun found himself secured in strong handcuffs. Two police constables suddenly appeared in the cabin doorway and Willett was hauled to his feet.

At the door he glared back over his shoulder and, for a moment, pulled himself free from his two jailers. He turned towards Nat, hatred and contempt still burning in his eyes.

'Don't think you've seen the last of me, boy,' he snarled.

The two policemen took him by the arms again. The door closed behind them and Bosun Willett was lost to view.

Chapter Ten

SEPTEMBER 1870

For the rest of the morning Nat sat in Mr Young's cabin, filling in all the tiny details which the Superintendent needed to know. Tommy Jenkins brought him food – just bread and cold meat – which he hungrily wolfed down. They could not speak but Tommy smiled at him and winked before he took away the plate and cup.

Emma and Miss Clarkson came in once or twice to see him and the Governess even managed the faintest of smiles. Emma was so excited she could hardly contain herself.

'I told you it would work out, Nat. I told you.'

Miss Clarkson took her away for her morning walk and Nat was left to Douglas Young's questioning. After an hour the Superintendent patted him on the knee and went out.

The room was warm in the morning sunlight and, shortly, Nat began to doze. For the first time in many weeks he felt secure and safe. He slept silently and dreamlessly.

He was awoken some time later by Douglas Young's hand on his shoulder. He started, as if suddenly realising where he was.

'Steady, Nat,' Young said. 'You're safe.'

He settled himself onto the sofa alongside the boy.

'I thought you might like to know about Jimmy and

his friends – considering how you saved the ship. And our lives as well, quite probably.'

Nat nodded, rubbing the sleep out of his eyes.

'Well, as you know, they were trying to set her on fire. They had some foolish notion about destroying the *Havannah* and escaping in the confusion. Where they thought they would go I really don't know.'

He paused and shook his head.

'Silly, stupid boys. Fire on any wooden ship is lethal. They would probably have died along with the rest of us.'

Nat shrugged. He didn't expect anybody – least of all Jimmy – to care about the *Havannah* as he did but he had always thought that the boy had an easy number. After all, he had been one of Bosun Willett's favourites.

'Yes,' said Mr Young when Nat gave voice to his thoughts, 'but it obviously wasn't enough to keep Jimmy happy. I suppose he just wanted his freedom. And Bosun Willett had become increasingly unpleasant over the past few months. Even Jimmy began to feel his wrath, I am told.'

Nat could well believe it. The knowledge that Nat was still alive and liable to inform on him would have kept the Bosun on the very edge of his temper. Woe betide anybody who crossed him.

'But what will happen to me now?' Nat asked. 'Everybody on board still thinks I stole the Bosun's knife.'

Young smiled and shook his head.

'No they don't. Jimmy has confessed. As you thought, the Bosun got him to plant the knife in your locker so that you'd be blamed. It seems the Bosun has always hated you, Nat, even before you stumbled on his little fraud. Goodness knows why. Perhaps he saw something hard and unafraid in you – something that wouldn't lie down and die. And that made him frightened because he'd come across something he couldn't squash. He couldn't beat the spirit out of you.'

The Superintendent paused, got to his feet and wandered over to the stern window of the ship. For several long moments he stared over the river and Bay.

'But he's gone now. Gone for good. He'll never set foot on the *Havannah* again. For that matter, neither will Jimmy and his cronies. They'll all be in Cardiff gaol within the hour and I think they're likely to stay there for a very long time.'

Nat felt the relief flood across his body. So it really was all over.

'And I can come back?' he smiled.

Young smiled. He turned to stare at the boy.

'Of course you can. We'll be pleased to have you. You'll make a ship's captain, yet, young Nat. We'll employ a new Bosun, somebody who doesn't use the rope end to teach.'

Nat knew that Young was serious. The man seemed different, more purposeful somehow – it was as if getting rid of Bosun Willett had been a turning point for him. Well, he would prove Mr Young right, Nat decided; he would study and work hard and he *would* become a ship's captain, no matter how long it took.

'Bosun Willett was a bad man, Nat,' Young continued. 'And I've been a weak one. I let him rule this ship because it kept things quiet and on an even keel. Nobody complained and I could get on with my teaching and my reading.'

He stared up at the rows of books which lined the cabin walls. Slowly he shook his head.

'There's more to life than reading, though. Miss Carpenter knew what the Bosun was like. Do you remember her visit, Nat? She said that I should get rid of him, then. But I didn't have the courage. It was easier to pretend, to pretend he didn't hate boys like you. To pretend that everything was all right.'

He paused and turned again to the wide stern window and its view of Penarth Head in the morning sunlight.

'But that's all over, Nat. I've found the courage now. You taught me that, by your example. There will never be fear again on this ship. I'm going to make the *Havannah* a safe and happy place. One day we'll solve the problem of poverty, Nat; one day boys like you will have the chance to live in peace and comfort. Without fear. And this is where it starts – here, today, on this ship. What do you say to that, eh Nat?'

There was no reply. Douglas Young turned quickly around and stared. Slowly, but with growing intensity, he began to laugh. Nat Thomas lay on the wide sofa – fast asleep.

THE SEVENTH SEAL

Julie Rainsbury

sb   £3.95   0 86383 960 6

Owen has to come to terms with the changes in his life.
It is not easy to accept a new step-mother and the move
from familiar, bustling Cardiff to an isolated cottage on
the west Wales coast.

He is helped to settle by Eleri and her mysterious
grandfather. With their encouragement and friendship,
Owen becomes fascinated by the sea – its power, its
dangers, and its ancient secret places.

HIGH WATER

Corinne Renshaw

sb   £4.95   1 85902 737 7

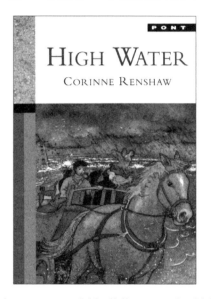

The Folly is a strange old building, perched high on the sea-wall, the first home to be flooded if the sea breaks through. In this eerie place, lives Joel, Rosie's friend – though friendship is not easy when families hate each other. Some old feud that no one will explain to a twelve year-old girl keeps Rosie's father angry and secretive. For Rosie, the worst of his secrets is his plan to send her to London to be brought up as a lady! She wishes with all her heart that something – anything – will stop her from leaving her home at High Water farm on the Monmouthshire levels.

DENNY

AND THE MAGIC POOL

Pamela Purnell

sb   £3.95   0 86383 990 8

When Denny's parents have problems, he goes to live with his
grandmother in Owen Street. She's kind, a brilliant cook and
sometimes seems to Denny even younger than his mother.
But even she is exasperated when Denny turns up plastered in
mud after 'going over the tide', walking the muddy shoreline of
the Taff mouth. Before the wild tide-fields are turned into
concrete and tarmac, Denny is determined to enjoy the natural
untidiness of it and can't keep away.
'Now listen to me, my boy. The river fascinates you. I know that.
But it's dangerous! It can change in a second – and sweep you
away. Denny – children have drowned in the Taff! You've been
warned all your life. You know about that treacherous old tide.
So why do you go there?'

FINDERS KEEPERS

Pamela Cockerill

sb   £4.50   1 85902 816 0

Jamie loses his bike *and* his father in the same week.
His bike is stolen and his father runs off with Wendy,
(Wonderbra, as Jamie calls her). As though surviving
his father's betrayal and his mother's mood swings is
not enough of a challenge, Jamie's life is further
complicated by the school bully. Then – a stroke of
good luck at last? – he finds a bike abandoned in the
grounds of Simnai, a big old house on his paper round.
Jamie rescues and restores it, but what is the mystery of
the bike's past? And where does Beth, the girl who has
moved into Simnai fit into things?